A
Jumpstart
To World Class Performance

Dave Garwood
and
Michael Bane

R. D. Garwood, Inc.
P.O. Box 28755
Atlanta, GA 30358-0755
(800) 241-6653
(404) 952-2976

A Jumpstart To World Class Performance

© 1988 Dogwood Publishing Company, Inc.
501 Village Trace, Building 9A
Marietta, GA 30067

ISBN 0-9621118-0-5

First Printing
Second Printing, 1989

Cover Design by Charles McShane Graphics
Illustrations by Ron Joudan

A
Jumpstart
To World Class Performance

Table Of Contents

Acknowledgements

We would like to express our sincere thanks to several people who gave us a high quality, quick response critique of **Jumpstart**. Their input was extremely valuable in fine-tuning the book.

We value and appreciate the input from our clients. David Cree, Director of ISD at Eastman Kodak; Joe Cox, former President and CEO at Centrilift; Roger Harker, President and CEO at Bently Nevada; Walt Henning, Vice President of Operations at Tone's, and John Paxton, Chairman and CEO at Intermec, were kind enough to take time from their busy schedules to give us their valuable feedback.

Our respected competitor, David Buker was a great sounding board and helped make this book a World Class effort.

Tom Womeldorff from CINCOM, gave us an excellent perspective from a CIM and software supplier point of view. Our thanks to all of them.

All of our business associates also supported this effort, and you will find their input all throughout the book. We want to especially thank John Civerolo and Chris Gray for their detailed review and critiques.

While we take full responsibility for everything you are about to read, we couldn't have done it without the help of all of these individuals. But most of the accolades go to you...the people in the real world of our manufacturing companies who work hard every day to make things better. Hopefully, each of you will see a little bit of your own operation in some of the chapters and chuckle. We are grateful for the opportunity that we have had to visit many of your plants, draw upon your experiences and pull this book together. We thank each and every one of you.

Dave Garwood
Michael Bane

Foreword

Competing to win! That's what this book is all about. The notion of winning the Competitive Race in the world of manufacturing companies isn't new.

> *"Not only the wealth, but the independence and safety of the country appear to be materially connected with the prosperity of manufacturers."*

Words of wisdom from a modern-day politician or industrialist? No. These are the words of Alexander Hamilton, a member of George Washington's cabinet when he gave his famous Report on Manufacturers.

We cannot escape the reality that a higher standard of living is dependent on people having extra income to purchase life's luxuries. And that means a competitive--and thus prosperous--manufacturing economy. Service industries and fast food outlets simply don't provide enough jobs that pay enough to give people an adequate discretionary income.

During the 1960s, American industry faced very little competition, and a certain complacency set in. Cost increases were simply passed on to the customers. Inflation was the excuse to rationalize price increases. The 70s brought us a clear vision of a stark reality...no business is immune to competition. Japan left a loud wake-up call. Dynasties fell quickly as an alarming--and increasing--amount of steel, automobiles and even consumer items, such as cameras and household electronics, were being made in Japan and sold worldwide.

The 1980s, though, have been a period of renewed optimism. Confidence has increased. A new thrust to leap out in front of the Competitive Race is evident. Unfortunately, the direction hasn't always been clear.

A Boston University survey recently revealed that, "In the early 1980s, confusion ruled the day as U.S. manufacturers tried to learn how to compete with tough new foreign competitors in a global market. Many companies went out of business. Others frantically looked for low-cost overseas suppliers and moved production offshore to get low-cost labor. But that quick fix strategy has gone by the board."

"Automate or evaporate" was a popular slogan, as some companies rushed out to the greenfield factory.

"Replace all the old equipment and brick buildings in the Rust Belt," was proposed by many.

Evidently, Lee Iacocca's experience was different. As he commented in a recent *Fortune Magazine* article, "It appears that our plant with the least automation and least investment is turning out the best quality."

What about computers? When IBM introduced their 1401 computer in the 1960s, computer horsepower to help run the everyday operations of a manufacturing business became practical. Since then, we've been struggling to harness that horsepower to make our factories more productive. Intuitively, many companies have suspected the computer can help, but most have been uncertain of how to effectively employ the computer.

Unfortunately, most of the applications ended up in accounting, replacing a few clerks while adding two programmers and a systems analyst. Profit improvements were marginal, at best. Most systems ended up in the category of *not good enough to use nor bad enough to throw out*. Twenty years later, we're still struggling with how to properly marry the power of the computer to crunch numbers and quickly communicate information with the skills of people to digest the data and make better decisions to run our businesses.

We've seen the frustration on the faces of executive management, middle management and the line worker as they peered over huge stacks of computer reports, swamped with data, but starved for information.

A lot of money has been spent, a lot of hard work done, a lot of project teams organized, but the results simply don't live up to their expectations.

Some companies focused on technical issues and forgot about the importance of people in the equation. Others hopped from one acronym or algorithm to another, always searching for a quick fix. The companies that have leapfrogged ahead in the Race have done it by taking a different approach...and they are enjoying successes...outstanding successes!

They rolled up their shirt sleeves and made the necessary changes in how they ran their business at the same time they installed the new hardware and software. They avoided looking for panaceas. They got everyone, from top to bottom in the organization, to buy in, to help, and to have fun doing it!

And that's the key.

The purpose of this book is to show you a clear path to follow to help you run your manufacturing business more competitively. We've written a book that is, we hope, easy, interesting reading and that reflects the real world. At times, we may step on a few toes and pierce a few egos. We mean no harm; we've only tried to tell the story as it really is.

More than just describing the problem, we give you a solution. **Jumpstart** identifies the solution by sharing with you the success that our hypothetical company enjoys in the end. We hope you enjoy reading the book. More importantly, we hope you hear the message loud and clear...immediately apply what you've learned and save thousands of jobs for the many men and women in industry. They deserve those jobs.

| Chapter One

Gray Days

The day Barbara Pilot showed up for work at the Kingsport plant was a gray one--low clouds and spitting rain threatened to turn into sleet at a moment's notice, while a cold north wind whipped dead leaves through the half-empty parking lot.

Welcome back, she thought, slamming shut the wooden door to the little brick reception building. Whatever happened to spring? She brushed a few scattered drops of rain off her canvas briefcase, crammed with confidential reports and two issues of competing computer magazines, and thought about San Diego, 85 degrees and the feel of the sun on her back.

Well, you wanted a challenge, she thought, while another part of her brain screamed, *a warm challenge, a warm challenge.*

The room, at least, was warm--hot, in fact, an electric heater with a clattering fan adding it's heat to what looked like an antique gas fireplace mounted half-way up one institutional green wall. The floor was brown and gray linoleum, with a worn path from the door leading to the plant from a second exit.

What a dump, she thought. This place hasn't been cleaned since the dawn of time--at least since the last time she'd been there. How come I didn't notice this when I interviewed in May?

In the spring, with the mountains alive with green and the air still crisp and clean, T&P Fabrications had seemed like just the ticket to shake her out of her Southern California doldrums, to shake off her brief stint in academia--no more wine spritzers, thank you, and to hell with tenure--and get back to doing something productive, to solving problems. T&P had been one of her first jobs out of college, stumbling into Production Planning with a degree in computer science. She'd lasted a couple of years before moving into larger and faster paced companies, riding the rising tide of computers across the country. She'd worked increasingly with computers and automation for a few years, finally accepting an offer to spend some time in the rarefied university atmosphere, researching the increased integration of computers into manufacturing.

But her manufacturing background made her something of a freak in a business school where the world according to MBA was the rule. One of her graduate assistants had summed it up pretty well when she told Barbara that she hoped to buy and sell factories, and with luck she would never ever have to set foot in one. Factories were icky.

Then, surprisingly, a call from T&P and, eventually, an offer to "take us into the next century" as Director of CIM, Computer Integrated Manufacturing. A blank slate, and enough capital to make something that worked.

A few rocky points, they'd told her, but nothing that couldn't be hammered out by a good problem solver.

And T&P--TeePee, as the locals dubbed the plant--had its share of problems. For a start, they had a ZAP mainframe that functioned--when it functioned, that is--pretty much as a very large, very expensive paperweight. Forget running the plant, buying and scheduling, whatever the thing was supposed to do. While she had been touring the computer center back in May she had personally witnessed the monster masticate an accounting program somebody was trying to feed it, then spit it out as confetti. At the time, it had seemed pretty funny.

"Give us a couple of months," Ed--"Fast Eddie to my friends"--Murdock, Director of MIS, had told her then, "and we'll have this sucker purring like an 1962 Chevy truck." Although Barbara's knowledge of cars was heavily slanted to things Japanese, she was sure that, in her limited experience, 1962 Chevy trucks didn't purr worth a darn.

The other problem--the reason, she suspected, that T&P had called her after six months of silence from the initial overtures--was that the business was heating up, getting more competitive, and somebody was going to be the loser in this race. T&P was looking for an edge.

"Barbara Pilot for Ed Murdock," she told the elderly man behind the desk. The guard's uniform looked two sizes too big, and his right pocket sagged under the weight of a shiny gold-plated badge. He smiled a surprisingly winning smile and spoke into an intercom--all it needs is a Dixie Cup on a string, she thought--motioning her to a cracked vinyl armchair near the heater. Some places never change.

"Mr. Murdock'll be along in a minute," he said, pushing her a laminated visitor's pass. "Just clip this on your jacket and you'll be fine."

The door from the plant side opened, admitting another blast of chilly--No, Barbara thought. Downright cold--autumn air and a middle-aged woman in a thick wool coat. She popped a laminated ID off her coat and handed it to the guard, who cranked up his smile to full blast.

"Fair to say we'll miss you, Mary Alice," the

guard said.

"Fair to say I'll miss you all, too," she replied, "but sometimes there's only so much you can shovel, you know?"

The elderly guard shook his head, and the woman looked toward Barbara.

"You comin' to work here?" she asked, just a touch too belligerently for Barbara's comfort. Barbara nodded.

"Great," the woman said, heading for the outer door. "Just what this place needs--another Suit. You take care, Tommy." Followed by another blast of cold air from both doors, as Fast Eddie Murdock plowed into the office.

"Barbara!" he said, extending a short, chubby arm, already pumping up and down. "Welcome aboard! And just in time, too!" He was already steering her out the door toward the main plant. "Feel like doin' a little buyin'?"

"Buying what?" she said, wrapping her coat tightly around her for the five or six steps to the main building.

"Computers, of course," said Fast Eddie. "Hardware, software, Tupperware. Just about every kind of 'ware they got, we need. We figure you're gonna get this straightened out once and for all. Get rid of all these tiny PCs' springing up like mushrooms in a cow pasture..." Eddie's chubby arms described a huge mushroom in the air.

"...At least, get 'em all tied together."

"What happened to the mainframe you've already got?" Barbara asked, only about half paying attention--Eddie's good ole boy schtick was strictly for visitors. He towed her through the main entrance (in substantially better shape than the guard house) into a fluorescent-lit corridor lined with glass display cases of T&P Products. There were plastic parts of all kinds--T&P parts found themselves in everything from CD players to automobile interiors. The 700 or so employees did everything from blend and color the plastic to injection molding to even some assembly of products--a cellular telephone cover assembly was shown. Looking spectacularly out of place in the center of the display cabinet was a bright red--fire engine red--model fire truck. Its red plastic doors faithfully opened, and there was a tiny black plastic crank that could be used to crank out the silver-colored plastic ladders. The fire truck, Barbara knew, had been T&P's first product back in the early 1960s, and a section of the plant still molded and assembled the plastic trucks, not only for kids, but for service station premiums as well.

"When I was here last time, you were getting that ZAP ready to purr like a Ford truck," she said.

"Chevy truck," Fast Eddie said, then his normal

good cheer faded a little. "What we did was we bought too small, then got the wrong software to boot. This MRP II program that corporate--heck, you saw we got bought right after we interviewed you, din'tja--made a super-de-luxe-get-it-crank-ing-or-else priority has eaten up that old machine. Heck, we were bein' *versioned* to death, you know. Version 6.0 didn't work, but they figured to fix it in 6.1, but it really took until 6.3, then there was another bug they were going to patch in 6.3.01 or some such. Then right in the middle of this MRP II thing, some guy comes down from USA headquarters in New Jersey with this other guy who wants to talk about quality. Quality this and quality that and quality all over the place. Which is pretty good, 'cept turns out what quality meant to these guys is charts and graphs and crunching numbers left and right. I'm not sure what all that's got to do with a good product, but don't ask me, I'm just the piano player around here. So I pulled a couple of guys off the murp stuff--"

"Murp?" Barbara said. He was called "Fast" be-cause of the way he talked, and she was almost exhausted just trying to keep up.

"--Murp. Rhymes with burp. Spelled M-R-P-I-I. Very boring people to invite to parties. Are real sincere and you keep expecting them to ask for money or something. So we got the guys started chewing up quality numbers, then jerked Tommy and Allison--you met 'em last time here, right?--off accounting and MRP II and added them to the charts and graphs folks. So MIS is already swamped--like we got nothing else to do, right?--and half my people are hauling in PCs to take some of the heat off the big machine. Next we get us a jitterbug..."

"Whoa!" Barbara shouted, out of breath from laughing. "A jitterbug? What the heck is a jitterbug?"

"In this here *particular* case, the jitterbug has an MBA from one of those fancy schools, a leather briefcase and a big time hankering for the Japanese. Jit, you know, Just-In-Time?" He looked at Barbara expectantly.

Barbara cracked up. "Just-In-Time people are jitterbugs?"

"Right," said Fast Eddie Murdock. "And they're planning on tearing up the plant something fierce, and nobody on the floor can figure out whatever for. Heck, they've even got the fire trucks screwed up. Not only that, but this morning Allison came in and said she wanted a raise for combat pay, 'cause yesterday she got caught between the murpers and the jitterbugs. She said if the quality people had been there, there probably wouldn't have been any survivors! Next week, we're going to post the match-ups on the bulletin board and start taking bets. And paper, you wouldn't believe the paper we're generating. Murper reports. Kanban cards with bar codes for the jitterbugs. Charts and graphs for the quality kids. Reams of paper. Stacks of paper. Mountains of paper. Well, heck, we're here..."

Chapter 2

Icebergs Ahead!

Barbara Pilot sighed heavily, shoved a stack of papers off to one side of her desk and lowered her head onto her arms. On the left side of that desk, a pale blue cursor blinked on the laptop computer she'd carried in from home to help with her planning. Heck of a Director of CIM, she thought wryly.

It had been a tough first three months. Her first meeting with J. Cleveland McKeever when she first started had definitely set the tone. T&P's CEO had struck Barbara as a man whose attentions were being pulled in far too many directions. He'd also struck Barbara as a very frustrated man.

"Don't get me wrong," he'd told her in that first meeting. "T&P makes a good profit. But it's getting tougher. We're having some delivery problems, and I don't like to hear our customers complain. We're also shipping most of our products at the last-minute, end-of-the-month crunch, and that shows no sign of letting up. And, of course, there's pressure from our benefactors at corporate to free up some capital from inventory, which we'd beefed up to offset some of the delivery problems."

J. Cleveland McKeever templed his hands.

"My people are working darned hard," he said. "Darned hard. But I'm not seeing results. We've got a bunch of people assigned to project teams, but they seem to just grind away, like a car that won't start. That's why I've come to you on this. I think if we tie all this hardware together, get our PCs networked and tied to the mainframe, get a new mainframe if we need the horsepower. Tie all that to the factory floor. Tie in Engineering through CAD/CAM. I think we might need to look at some computer-controlled equipment on the shop floor, maybe even hire a couple of robots. Whatever we look at, though, we have to see some results..."

Barbara had smiled winningly, and J. Cleveland McKeever almost blushed.

"Sorry," he had said. "It's all these speeches I keep making. Stockholders. New owners. Corporate dog-and-pony show. New York. New Jersey. Switzerland. Now I seem to make speeches at the drop of a hat."

Barbara had begun working on a spreadsheet--

the meticulously constructed model of one segment of TeePee's output, the plastic fire trucks. Her spreadsheet told a story she didn't want to hear.

"Cheer up," said Fast Eddie Murdock, easing into her sparsely decorated cubicle like a tugboat nudging a floating dock. "The good news is we've got a meeting with The Man in 15 minutes..."

"And the bad news," said Barbara, her head still down on her desk, "is that we can't even build the damn fire trucks."

Fast Eddie stopped short.

"Why can't we build the damn fire trucks?" he asked. "You know how those things are like the office pets. Jeez, if we worried as much about our other products as those fire trucks, we'd be billionaires..."

"We're out of THX-17-2305-Xs," said Barbara.

"I am awed with your memory from the dim old days," Fast Eddie said, bowing slightly. "For those of us earthlings still working around here, what is a THX-whatever?"

"Axles," she replied, resuming her walk toward the executive offices. "Little pieces of steel rod that you stick the truck tires on. I got an emergency-crash-pay-attention-to-me memo two days ago that said the truck line was down due to a computer glitch. Since I've been kind of wandering around getting a feel for the place before I make any recommendations, I thought I'd check into this particular problem. So I called up the inventory record, and it says we have 10,000 of the suckers lying around. Yesterday, I went down to the shop floor to ask where they were and ran smack into Eldon..."

"You met the Man Mountain!"

Barbara laughed. Eldon Sims was about as hard to miss as a subcontinent. He waddled when he walked, wore suspenders that could probably be cited by OSHA as insufficient to hold up that much bulk and was reputed to be the only one of TeePee's 700 employees who actually knew what was going on at any given time. Actually, what was going on was that everything was "on-order." "In this department," Eldon pontificated to everyone in earshot, "you're never right. The trick is to make sure you're never wrong."

"What pearls of wisdom did the Man Mountain have to say?" Fast Eddie said.

"Axles are on-order, along with roughly everything else in the plant. I take it Eldon constantly orders a little of everything?" Barbara said.

"Cover your not-unsubstantial posterior," Eddie replied. "Eldon wrote the book on coverage."

"Anyhow, there was some kind of screwup. Engineering upgraded and we started using three axles and six tires instead of two axles and four tires. We got tires out the wazoo, but nobody thought to get enough axles."

"What about Purchasing?"

"Axles are as-required, you know, marked A/R on the bill of material." Barbara said. "They're not part of the formal system, such as it is. I guess they send a stock boy down to the Axle Store every time they need a bunch of them."

They reached the door to the executive offices. Before Eddie could open the door, Barbara stopped him.

"Here's my question," she said. "If we don't know what's in the stuff we make, and we don't know what we've got in inventory to put in the stuff we make, how are we going to make the stuff, anyway?"

"Welcome," Fast Eddie said, "to American industry."

The conference room was newly refurbished, nondescript Swedish and smelled of lemon oil and coffee. Seated at the pale oak table was The Man himself, J. Cleveland McKeever, whose father had started T&P back in the Psychedelic Sixties, right about the time Dustin Hoffman was advised that the future was, indeed, "Plastics," and who'd carried the plastics torch through much of the Uncertain Eighties, and, he sincerely hoped, on into the Prosperous Nineties. Arrayed around

Keever was the leader of the Quality Initiative team, Jason Rice, a slim intense man in a brown corduroy jacket who was constantly badgering MIS for four-color graphics and charts that looked like a Dali representation of a black hole, and, Barbara knew, the head jitterbug, Teresa Ann Townsend, with a fresh MBA on top of an engineering degree from Stanford. She looked like Malcomb Forbes' vision of a nun, and the fact that she was almost ten years Barbara's junior didn't make things any easier. Barbara had speculated that Teresa Ann probably had neither furniture in her apartment nor food in her refrigerator, not wanting to maintain a personal inventory. The murp contingent was at the opposite end of the oak table from The Man, no doubt a bad sign, Barbara figured, for Sam Medley, who'd been trying to get the MRP II program really cranking for more than a year. The harder he cranked, she'd heard them say on the shop floor, the deader it got. Still, for all her less-than-kind characterizations, they were not a bad lot to work with--at least, as long as you didn't end up in the same room with the whole batch.

"Barbara, Ed, glad you could make it on such short notice," The Man said. J. Cleveland loved his weekly meetings. Each meeting lasted precisely 20 minutes, and anybody who had questions was met with an expression that fell somewhere between a smile and a grimace, the face of an adult whose 14-year-old had just asked whether Wisconsin was in the United States. There weren't many questions.

It was clear to Barbara that The Man's attention wasn't all in Kingsport--he was fighting battles in other corporate wars on other fronts, and Barbara found that lack of total attention irrationally irritating. She had to remind herself at times that this was the same man who had taken the family business public, then negotiated the leveraged buyout minefield, arranged a sale to an international conglomerate and, although now very rich, opted to keep not only his job, but T&P fairly autonomous.

"I think what we're all interested in," The Man was saying, "is when we can expect the recommendations on the new software and hardware. It's no secret that I'm more than a little frustrated. Over the last 18 months, we've launched three separate programs--MRP II, JIT and the Quality Initiative. To be frank, I've heard a lot of talk, but seen darn little bottom line results. That's where you come in, Barbara.

"I think it's hardly a secret that we're floundering on these programs"--he paused and looked around the room, but nobody avoided his gaze-- "and it's time to get on with it. We need some kind of jumpstart to get these programs going again, maybe some new hardware or software that's going to tie all these different programs together."

Barbara had been waiting for this one. That was her job, why they'd come back to a systems engineer with academic credits and a couple of articles on "Computerizing The Factory Of The Future." She had spent the three months since she started at T&P talking to Finance, talking to Product and Manufacturing Engineering, talking to Purchasing. She'd spent time being wooed by software and hardware vendors, visiting other plants, slogging through stacks of home-grown code.

And she was confused.

"Sixty days," she heard a voice she suddenly recognized as her own blurt out. Her commitment. Fast Eddie looked amazed. Jason Rice actually seemed to shrink in his seat from relief, and even Teresa Ann Townsend gave a nod of approval.

"Excellent," said J. Cleveland McKeever. "I don't suppose you can give us any preliminary budget estimates, can you? Our benefactors in Switzerland would like to know how much they're going to have to twist the little banker gnomes for."

"I'd really rather not say just yet," Barbara said. "The verdict isn't totally in."

Exactly four minutes later--20 minutes on the button--the meeting came to an end.

"Sixty days," said Fast Eddie, heading back down the hall. "I didn't know you were that far along."

"Well, actually, I'm not," Barbara said, looking straight ahead. She stopped, turned and looked at the head of MIS. "Have you ever thought that maybe it wasn't the computers?" she began, taking a deep breath. "Look at the fire trucks. I've got no problems with the hardware on that point. I can bring up inventory records on the CRT that show 10,000 axles, only there aren't 10,000 axles. There aren't any axles. MRP II is supposed to tell us when to go out and buy axles, except that axles aren't on the bill of material, because Eldon says why would you put a little ole thing like a piece of steel on the bill of material and clutter it up? Usually, he orders a bunch of everything anyway. Engineering agrees with Eldon, only they're not sure how many axles they're going to put on next year's fire truck. You know Fred Thomas down in Sales? Just for the heck of it, I called him and asked how many fire trucks we were going to need next year, and he started laughing. Told me he was going to cast the entrails of a chicken and get back to me. And this is for the fire trucks! Think about the frame assembly for the professional VCRs. The contract with Panasonic on those CD player assemblies. How am I supposed to program around all that?"

"Beats me," Fast Eddie said. "But in 60 days you're going to tell me."

She smiled weakly. "I work better with a deadline."

"And by the way," Eddie added with a grin. "Speaking as the head of a corporate MIS department with 20 years' experience to the new Director of Computer Integrated Manufacturing, *never* say it's not the machine."

Barbara laughed.

Chapter Three

Workouts

Sixty days, huh?"

"Sounds like a prison sentence, doesn't it?" Barbara said between clenched teeth. She methodically pushed the bar of the Nautilus bench press machine up for the twelfth and final time, then sat up, sweat pouring down her face and soaking the TeePee Softball Aces t-shirt she wore over her leotard. The small woman straddling the leg curl machine opposite Barbara broke into a laugh and tossed Barbara a towel.

"It is a sentence!" said Laura Meyers, grabbing a second towel from the weight bench and wrapping it around her shoulders. "What on earth made you give yourself a deadline like that? Jeez, it's not as if the Suits--present company excluded, of course--haven't had plenty of time to get everything this messed up."

Barbara shrugged, twisting around to wipe the sweat off the machine. The little gym was, if anything, a sign of T&P's good faith. They'd taken two unused storerooms, Victorian artifacts with high ceilings and concrete columns in the middle of the room, knocked out a wall, and furnished a surprisingly complete fitness center, with used but refurbished Nautilus machines, free weights and an electronic rowing machine that never worked right.

Barbara had found the gym her second day and had since never missed a chance to work out. She'd also found Laura Meyers, one of the floor supervisors on the VCR chassis assembly line. Laura was short with spiky blonde hair and biceps that looked like she could punch as well as talk. And if she did punch, Barbara figured, she sure as heck wouldn't pull any, since she didn't in any other area. More than one manager, usually a newcomer, had his throat taken out when he dared tread on her turf.

And her workers loved her for it. Hanging over her desk in the cluttered, dusty cubicle next to the VCR line was not only a framed picture of her son, in his first year at the University of Virginia, but a plaque with pictures of 25 employees on it, a gift from those employees when cutbacks forced their layoff, over Laura's furious opposition a couple of years back. *Thanks*, a brass plate on the bottom of the plaque read.

"People just don't realize how important time is," Barbara said. "We dance around and we dance around, and the next thing we know there are six companies in Taiwan selling to our next door neighbors..."

"Ah," Laura said, twisting her shoulders in a long stretch that had joints popping, "the frustrated schoolteacher. Just buy 'em their damn new computer and be done with it, why don't you."

"It's not the computer."

"Well, of course it's not the computer!" Laura countered. "What does that have to do with anything?"

"What do you mean, 'Of course it's not the computer?'" Barbara said, interested. The general consensus among the upstairs managers was that the shop floor people were somewhere between willful children and sullen adolescents, needing a benign managerial hand to show them where the machines were every day. It wasn't a *stated* policy, mind you, and no one would say anything that crass out loud. But Barbara had noticed that when the floor supervisors or even someone like Eldon Sims òr Floyd the Fixer ventured into the administrative regions and started talking, people's eyes began to glaze over.

Laura stood up and began pacing around the gym, empty except for the two women.

"All right," she said. "Look at this. We build chassis for three types of recorders, right?

Professional stuff. Expensive. All just a little bit different. No big deal, except that the idiots in Sales don't know a darn thing about what they're selling. They got projections that are pretty much like weather reports, you know--if it don't rain, it'll be clear, but if it do rain, it'll be wet."

She punctuated each "rain" with a thrust of her hips, and Barbara had to laugh.

"Then these guys in Purchasing, and don't get me wrong, some of my best friends are in Purchasing, although I wouldn't want my daughter to marry one. Anyway, these guys take the Sales forecast, such as it is, and figure out how to buy as much of the wrong stuff as possible. You know, we still have about twenty jillion pieces of a chassis that Sony obsoleted two years ago. Got a good price on 'em, though, I'll bet they did."

"So how do you figure what to make?" Barbara, somewhere between amused and puzzled, asked.

"That's easy," Laura said. "Whatever's easiest. The stamper stamps, the riveter rivets and the trimmer trims. As long as we keep making *something* all the time, everyone upstairs is happy, more or less."

"You don't sound all that happy."

Laura gave an elaborate shrug of her shoulders, and Barbara could see the muscles ripple.

"My people aren't fools," she began, then snapped her towel against the wall of the gym.

"They don't give a damn about us. The only time they listen to us is when we threaten them," she said. "Couple of months before you came, what's his name, the murp, the MRP II guy came down with a new plan for my line. You know, part of my line moves pretty quick, we keep adding parts to the main chassis and shoving stuff through. So he says he's been studying my line, reading the murp book or something, and according to him each point on the line was a subassembly, and each one of those subassemblies needed a part number. And to make MRP II work, we needed to keep track of all those subassemblies, log 'em in and out of inventory, file a bunch of reports, a pile of paperwork for every person on the line. And then he started talking about bar code readers and computer terminals to keep track of all the part numbers and subassemblies..."

Barbara was more than a little interested. She'd heard from Sam Medley, the project manager, that the MRP II project was stalled because of "software problems" and "attitude problems of some personnel," and she had wondered what on earth that was all about. She even had it on her list to find out what the last two dozen or so memos really meant.

She'd run into Floyd the Fixer, the Hot List man, the day before, and even he had cracked a joke about the murps. When Barbara had asked whether Floyd thought the MRP II program was important, Floyd had smiled his ferret grin. "Do you see J. Cleveland down here?" he said. "Do you see any of the Suits down here working on any of these high-speed new programs? What does that tell you?"

Barbara admitted that it told her a lot.

"So what did you tell Sam Medley?" Barbara asked Laura Meyers.

"Well," Laura replied, "it was like with drugs, you know. I just said no. I asked him, 'What would you rather us do, make these things, or fill out paper about making these things?' He didn't have a good answer. Bar code readers! Give me a break."

Laura stopped pacing and threw her arms up dramatically, and Barbara could see why her people were so loyal and why management hated to see her coming. Still, Barbara had the germ of an idea, a way to present at least *something* of value in 60 days.

"I want to spend some time with you on the shop floor," Barbara said. "That's where I'm weakest, but that's where the problems seem to be showing up."

"We're the trap at the bottom of the drain," Laura said. "Engineering makes a mistake, Purchasing makes a mistake, Accounting makes a mistake, all of 'em end up with us. It's always our fault. Want to come down for lunch?"

"Actually, what I had in mind was more of a week or so," Barbara said.

"Can you do that?"

"I have, and I quote from the The Man, 'Whatever you need to get the job done,'" Barbara said, "and I think I need some time on the shop floor."

"I've seen you on the shop floor a lot," Laura shrugged.

"And it's like visiting a foreign country," Barbara countered, maybe a bit more sharply than she intended. "Half of what's wrong with this place is that it's like an armed camp--the Suits versus the shop, the jitterbugs versus the quality clones, MRP II saves the whole world, or, my personal favorite, MIS takes on all comers. We might as well have a bulletin board at the main entrance listing the day's bouts and posting yesterday's scores!"

Barbara waved her own hands to emphasize her point, successfully wrapping her soggy towel around the top bar of the shoulder press machine. Laura burst out laughing.

"All right, all right! If you can clear it with the guys upstairs, I'll be your guide through the belly of the beast. One favor, though," Laura said.

"Name it."

"No suits, okay?"

Chapter Four

An Ugly Intrusion Of Reality

The excursion to the shop floor had been an education for Barbara--especially regarding the topic of education.

"Education?" said the sweating man taking a ten-minute break from the trimming machine. He slipped his hands from the gloves that held them out of the machine's reach, then pushed his New York Mets baseball cap back from his face.

"We got all flavors of education here, Miss Barbara," he said. "Which particular flavor do you want?"

True to her word, Barbara Pilot was not wearing a suit. In her jeans and sweatshirt and running shoes, she looked like 90 percent of everyone else on the line. Laura Meyers, also true to her word, had turned her line over to her second in command and was on "special assignment" as "tour guide."

"That's what I am," she said. "Visit the wild, unexplored territory of the shop floor."

Laura had started with her own line.

"Go ahead, Peter," Laura was saying. "Show Barbara the archives."

Peter, the trimmer with the Mets cap, grinned like a little kid and wiped some of the plastic flecks off his face.

"Step right this way," he said. He led the way through two small riveters and a machine that punched parts out of a larger sheet of plastic. Next to the toolroom was a filing cabinet that Barbara figured had seen better days--probably somewhere around 1936. It was olive drab and scraped to bare metal in places, and, judging by the dents, it had been used to try and dissuade a charging rhino sometime in its past. There was a yellowed paper sign taped to the side that read, "KEEP OUT! THIS MEANS YOU! I'M NOT JOKING! SIGNED LAURA."

Peter pulled open the bottom file drawer, which creaked and groaned like a pensioner on a bicycle. Then he stepped back and gave a brief bow.

"Tah dah!" he said with a flourish. "The professional VCR chassis line historical archives!"

The drawer was filled with baseball hats and what looked like party favors.

Barbara bent over and pulled out a bright yellow baseball hat almost on the top of the pile. The front of the hat had a smiling happy face on it and an inscription that read, "MRP II Is Coming!" She'd seen one just like it hanging on a hook in Sam Medley's office. The hat was partially tangled with what looked like a small banner, which Laura reached over and unfurled. "Continuous Improvement," it read.

"I kinda like that one," Peter, a regular participant in local karate matches, said. "Very Zenish."

"Everybody chips in," Laura said. "Whenever we get sent to class, or someone comes around passing stuff out, we save one for the archives. Sort of like educational souvenirs."

Barbara reached back into the drawer and found a hat stenciled "Management By Objective." Another read, "Quality YES! Rejects NO!" A crumpled red baseball hat stuffed in the back exhorted, "Job Safety Is Up To You!" One enigmatically read "84 Percent And Counting!"

"What's that mean?" Barbara asked.

"Who knows," Peter replied.

Peter headed back to his machine, and Laura closed up the archives.

"How many hats are in there?" Barbara wanted to know.

"Oh, fifteen or twenty," Laura said. "I've been here about 16 years, and we get one a year, just about. Used to be kind of like the flu, you know, a bug goes around and everybody gets sick for a couple of weeks. The last 18 months, though, have been killers. Seems like for a while I was spending every Saturday in classes--MRP, JIT, one or the other. Then we had two of those big what they called 'Super Class' sessions with those two hot-shot consultants from California. The quality guy got to shouting and waving his arms so good I thought they were going to pass a collection plate!"

"You had to spend Saturday in classes?" Barbara asked. When Laura shook her head yes, Barbara said, "Did you get paid?"

"Sure," the other woman said. "We got paid in donuts, coffee and a new hat for the archives. Was I excited!"

"Was everybody as excited as you were?"

"What do you think?" Laura said. "And forget about asking questions. If we asked any questions, we'd *still* be there. Plus, who wants to look like an idiot in front of those hot-shot outsiders? If it's so *damned* important that we've got to learn it, then why isn't it important enough to learn it on company time?"

That was, Barbara thought, a not unreasonable question. By then, the two women had gotten back to Peter's machine. With his safety glasses and dust mask on, he looked something like a tanned insect.

"Look at it this way," Peter said through his dust mask, giving his voice the faint buzz of a lousy stereo speaker. Each one of these programs is like a boat, you know, the New Idea Boat. There's the MRP II boat, the JIT boat, a quality boat, and now you're the captain of the CIM boat. And here I am standing on the dock, and these guys are shouting, 'Jump aboard! Jump aboard!' So I smile and wave and put one foot on the boat. But I keep one foot on the dock, and when that boat starts to pull away, I raise that foot on the boat, and I think, 'Two feet on the dock.' I stay right there on the dock. Know why? Cause there's a Bermuda Triangle out there, and it eats them boats right up. And I notice that the people who shouted 'Jump aboard! Jump aboard!' don't seem to be around here any more, and I'm still here, running this trimmer..."

"You're a regular philosopher, Peter," said Laura. "If you could run that machine half as well as you can talk, you'd be rich by now."

"Not the whip, Mistress!" Peter said in mock distress, slipping his hands back in the safety gloves. He nodded wryly at Barbara and began finishing parts.

The two women continued to walk down through the plant, leaving Laura's line and heading to another section of the factory, where the beads of raw material were mixed, blended, melted and formed into sheets of plastic.

"These guys couldn't get product out on time if their lives depended on it," Laura said derisively. Barbara had heard the same thing from other supervisors in Manufacturing, whose lines either slowed to a crawl or shut down when the sheets of plastic weren't ready when Manufacturing needed them.

The two women turned the corner and almost crashed into "Red" Dunn, the plant manager, who was headed toward the administrative offices with a stack of papers in his hands.

"Whoa!" he said, his black work shoes making a scraping noise on the concrete floor. "Sorry. I get so fired up sometimes I need bumpers."

Barbara and Laura gave the obligatory laugh. Barbara had mixed feelings about Red, whose hair, she figured, must have been red before it turned mostly grey. He'd come up from the bottom, a line worker on the fire truck line, and had put in almost 20 years at T&P. "He's got an attitude problem," Eddie Murdock had told her. "If it's new, he hates it." And Red Dunn had been fiercely disapproving of the new programs: "If it ain't broke," he was fond of announcing at the slightest provocation, "don't fix it." He was also fiercely protective of the shop floor. "We do our jobs," he'd told Barbara one afternoon. "If the other departments would do theirs, we wouldn't have all the problems we're having." Seeing Barbara, whom Red perceived as the new thorn in his side, was like waving the proverbial red flag in front of a bull.

"As long as I've run into you two..." he began, and Barbara mentally groaned. "These are more reports for the boys upstairs on how things are going down here. I just don't know, Barbara. I'm worried. I mean, are these things ever going to work? Maybe they're great at Sony or Panasonic or Hewlett Packard or Toyota, but do they really apply here at all? I mean, we're not one of the big guys here. And is it even really worth it? I mean, things have been going pretty good here for years..."

Laura groaned out loud, and Red Dunn turned as red as his hair once was.

"You aren't exactly knocking yourself out for this stuff either," he said to Laura. "And I'd say that's pretty smart. You've got a pretty good job here right now, but who knows what you'll have when we finish M-R-P-ing and J-I-T-ing and T-Q-C-ing and"--he looked pointedly at Barbara--"C-I-M-ing. Maybe there won't be any employees here at all except the guy who comes in first thing in the morning to turn the automated factory on."

Laura started to say something, but Barbara put a hand on her shoulder. "Do a lot of people on the shop floor feel the same way you do?" Barbara asked.

"A whole lot," Red Dunn said. "I'd even say a majority of them. These new hot-shot ideas come and go, but nothing ever changes. They're just fads, like paisley shirts. And on that note, I'll be heading upstairs..."

As the plant manager headed toward Administration, Barbara began talking, almost to herself.

"They're neither for nor against," she said. "But you'd never know it until somebody like good old never-shut-up Red opens his mouth."

"Sort of like the old Richard Nixon days, you know," Laura replied. "Remember the Silent Majority? Well, that's what we got here."

The head of the mixing and blending section of Manufacturing, named Lowrey, was as frustrated as everyone else. The vendors who supplied the plastic beads and various agents blended to create the sheets were nothing short of Iranian rug merchants, figuring every way on earth to run some kind of scam. The vendors didn't deliver on time, and when they did deliver, half the stuff was the wrong material, the wrong colors, the wrong concentrations. Over a period of years, he'd worked with Purchasing to come up with what amounted to a "nuke them before they nuke us" policy of dealing with the vendors--get multiple quotes for each item, play one vendor off against another and go to the mat for pennies. Because they were uncertain of vendor delivery, everything was scheduled earlier--if you needed it on Labor Day, ask for delivery on the Fourth of July, then you had a shot at getting it on time. They also kept increasing the order quantity, which only made sense, Barbara was told, because that way you got them cheaper. "If there's a standard of one dollar, and we can get them for ninety cents if we order 100,000, that's a ten-cent-per-piece savings," Purchasing told Barbara. "Think of the money we're saving! Besides, we need to get a lot, because some of the ones we do get are bad. This way, we can always sort through and find enough good ones."

Laura introduced Barbara to a friend of hers on the plastics line, then went looking for a cup of coffee.

Her friend, James Jeffrey Jones--J.J. to friends and enemies alike--was a strapping man with a bald head the color of aged ebony. Ten years before, he'd been a linebacker for the University of Tennessee until an extremely painful elbow, of all things, canceled chances for a pro career. "I wasn't much for painkillers," he'd explained. His particular position was expediter with Purchasing, and he'd laughingly told Barbara that he was sorry he hadn't brought his football helmet with him to work for T&P.

"Listen," he said to her. "Contrary to popular belief, I'm not one for sports analogies. But vendors *are* the opposing team. We nail them or they nail us."

Barbara didn't respond. And J.J. looked sheepish.

"Okay, okay, so maybe it's not the Super Bowl. But the way you get your prices manageable, the way you get material in the shop, is by playing one off against the other," he said.

"What about single sourcing?" Barbara asked. She'd read how some of the most progressive companies had boiled their many vendors down to one for a single material, making that vendor a partner instead of an adversary. J.J. snorted, a sound, Barbara imagined, much like a small, localized thunderstorm. The vendors must be terrified, she thought.

"Single sourcing?" he said. "How badly do you want product out of this line? Man, if we single-sourced even a couple of our raw materials or chemicals, you'd have more luck buying sheets of plastic as blue light specials at K-Mart than getting them off this line!"

"But why?" Barbara pushed. In her months at TeePee, she'd heard "because" and "that's the way we do things here" so many times she was prepared to slug J.J. if she heard it again. Instead, the big man folded into what seemed to be a tiny chair and ran his fingers through an imaginary head of hair.

"Look," he said. "Everything here is on an air-raid standard. We come to work in the morning, somebody blows the siren and we all dive for cover."

Take, he added, for instance, this morning.

"At 9:01 this morning, Floyd the Fixer--you know Floyd?"

Barbara nodded. Everybody knew Floyd. He was half of the Floyd and Eldon Show--Eldon Sims ordered a little of everything, and Floyd the Fixer was the Hot List man, the expediter, the man who knew the status of everything, what was *really* going on. He was skinny and looked like a ferret and always had a thoroughly chewed pencil behind his ear and a dog-eared yellow legal pad in his hands. He always wore cheap, too-baggy jeans and $100 Reebok running shoes that he had to replace every six months or so. His clothes might be thrift store specials, but he had to be able to move *fast*.

"So Floyd comes running in with the day's Hot List. The fire truck parts, God bless the little beggars, line is running low, so we need to run some one-half centimeter red sheet. No problem, except we use a special dye for that particular sheet--you know we got 11 shades of 'red' here?" J.J. shook his massive head.

"I send Floyd back to check on the dye, and he calls back in about six seconds to say there ain't none," J.J. continued.

"What's the inventory record say?" she asked.

"Why would I check the inventory record?" J.J. asked, genuinely puzzled. "So I call four of our suppliers to look for the red dye. Then it's like a poker game. They all got the dye, or can run a short batch for us, but, because it's crash and burn notice, they want to hold us up on price. WWF Chemicals has the best price, but their dyes are always just a shade off-color. If I'm in a bind--like now--I'll take the risk, what the heck, orangish-red fire trucks. But I'll try to figure a way to hammer them down, maybe play 'em off a couple of other companies."

"It seems like a huge waste of effort..." Barbara began.

"It is a huge waste of effort," replied Laura, who'd come back with the coffee and was standing off the side, listening. "He hasn't even told you about the set-up problems and the order quantity weirdness."

"It only makes sense, Laura," J.J. said. Turning to Barbara, he said, "When we get the dye, we'll run 5,000 sheets of red half-centimeter, because that's the most economical run."

"That's six months worth of fire trucks," Laura added. "Unless, of course, Engineering decided to go from half-cm to quarter-cm sheets."

"Will they?" Barbara asked.

"Well," said J.J., laughing, "we've still got 4,600 sheets of 3/8-cm from four years ago! Remember--think air raid!"

Chapter Five

Back To School

Barbara Pilot sat in the offices of The Man the morning after her week on the shop floor with Laura Meyers. She'd decided to exercise her initiative and go to the top for an overview of the corporate policy on education. Much to her surprise, The Man himself stepped out of his office while she was making an appointment and invited her in.

"Do you have any idea how much this corporation spent on education last year?" J. Cleveland McKeever said a quick greeting. He ushered her to an overstuffed leather chair facing his antique desk. There was a stuffed moosehead on the wall that everyone in MIS called Einstein Junior, or E.J. for short. Everyone suspected that J. Cleveland's father had bored it to death some afternoon years back.

"That's one of the reasons I wanted to talk to you," she said.

"Well, last year, we spent a total of $25,000 on

education in MRP II, JIT and TQC, not counting our purchase of two video libraries" he said. "I think that's a significant number."

"It's definitely a good start," Barbara began, then stopped and started over. "I don't know. Actually, it may not even be a good start. What did we get for that money, Mr. McKeever?"

J. Cleveland McKeever templed his hands and began methodically using the tip to scratch his nose, a motion commonly credited by second floor Man-Watchers with signifying deep thought.

"Other than the obvious problem of training new operators, what does the education program have to do with your recommendations on new hardware and software?" he asked.

"I'm beginning to think it has everything to do with those recommendations," she said. "In fact, I'm beginning to be convinced that the problem I was hired to solve has a lot more to do with the education program than with automating the factory. Mr. McKeever, I don't think we need to recable the plant or even bring in the robots."

"I'm sure our benefactors, the gnomes, will be glad to hear that," The Man said mildly, leaning back in his leather armchair, which creaked loudly. "On what do you base your suppositions?"

Boy, thought Barbara, *this has got to be the most clever way I've come up with to get myself booted out of a job. Hired to cable the place. Tell 'em they don't need it. For this I have a Masters degree.*

"We're asking," she began hesitantly, leaning forward and tapping her fingers on the edge of her boss's desk, "for hardware solutions to all our problems, but I'm not sure we're even correctly stating the problems..."

She paused to collect her thoughts, and The Man nodded his head with encouragement. Of course, Barbara thought, the nod could just as well mean, "Go ahead and hang yourself..."

"We're geared to think in terms of a hardware solution," she said. "Heck, *I'm* geared to think in terms of a hardware solution. That's what I do, and what I was hired to do here..."

J. Cleveland McKeever nodded his head.

"We wouldn't even flinch at spending one or two million on hardware and software," Barbara continued. "But we start counting pennies when it comes to people. "In the companies I looked at during my stint in the university, the vast majority of the benefits of new programs were coming not from the software and hardware, but from the people."

"Where is the flaw in our education system?" he challenged.

"Well," she said, "it all seems to be geared toward learning some acronym. Learn MRP II, learn TQC, learn JIT, learn CIM. Or learn to use the new software package."

"Isn't that what we want our people to do?" he said.

"Not really," Barbara said. "At least, I don't think so. I mean, we might need new hardware, or a new software package might help. But that's not *the* solution. What we want them to do is do their jobs differently than they do them now. You know, change their behavior. And that's more than just learning about CIM or JIT or reading a new computer report."

"Give me an example," said J. Cleveland McKeever.

"Okay, let's look at our special promotional orange fire trucks due out second quarter next year..."

Barbara knew about his soft spot for the fire trucks.

"I expect those to be a bright spot for us second quarter. In fact, we need those second quarter sales to generate enough profit to keep corporate out of our hair," J. Cleveland replied. "In fact, I've instructed our Sales people to get on a couple of national promotions with two of the major oil companies."

"Sales said if they push, they ought to be able to move three or four times as many fire trucks as usual for that time of year, so I asked the people in Manufacturing about additional capacity planning for the special promotion. They just laughed at me," Barbara said. "Rumors. Forget it. Never happen. If I believed in the Sales forecast, I probably believed in the Easter Bunny as well..."

J. Cleveland snorted.

"I went over to Engineering and talked to Ann Rosetti, who's the project manager on fire trucks," Barbara continued. "She's really excited, because they've got some design innovations that should lower costs on the new fire trucks by around 16 percent and increase quality..."

"That's interesting," The Man said.

"And they should be able to get everything hammered out in time for third quarter delivery," Barbara said.

"Third quarter?" he almost shouted. "But we have a special promotion going. I've already communicated our projected revenue increases to our benefactors and our stockholders. We're *committed* to second quarter delivery."

"Nobody knows that," Barbara said. "Or, at least, not everybody. I talked to Purchasing about the orange dye we'll need for the plastic-- it's not something we normally use. They hadn't been informed of anything yet. Since I told her, Alyse Anderson is scrambling around looking for the dye. She made a couple of calls and found out the dye is a special order and available in 13 weeks lead time. That means we should have ordered the dye two weeks ago. She also suggested that when we do order, we only order 80 percent of what Manufacturing asks for, since their capacity planning is, 'strictly Disneyland.'"

J. Cleveland McKeever was quiet for a moment, then very angry.

"That's exactly what I meant," he said, visibly frustrated. "Lots of talk, not much action. We've spent a lot of dollars on these project teams, on education, on hardware, on everything, and we're still running the business off the back of an envelope. Nothing changes. Business as usual."

"Lots of talk, but no communication. Nobody believes anybody, and all the numbers are suspect," she said. "But my point is that kind of problem can't be solved with a new computer or a network of PCs or automated machinery. Nobody seems to be working to the same plan. There's no integration of the Sales plan with the operation of the company. No one part of the factory seems to have the slightest idea what the other part is doing..."

"But you have to understand the unique situation we're in," he said, still visibly flustered. "We blend and mix our own plastics, some of which we sell in small lots. We inject and mold parts, some of which we sell. We build subassemblies for other manufacturers and we have a small toy line. We can't make to stock, and how do you forecast a make-to-order business? How many other companies do all that and have our unique problems? How can we educate around that?"

"Before I went back to those ivory towers," Barbara said, "I worked with several other companies after I left T&P, as I'm sure you know..."

The Man nodded.

"One of those companies was a defense contractor who made missile guidance parts," Barbara said. "Another made really pricey women's lingerie. A third made breakfast cereal. I've just spent a week on the shop floor, and the problems those people described to me are identical to the problems I heard at the missile factory, at the cereal company and even at the place where they made underwear! We may be unique, but I don't think our problems are..."

"So you're suggesting that if our problems aren't unique," J. Cleveland McKeever picked up, leaning forward, "neither are the solutions. At this point, I'm inclined to think we have nothing to lose; clutch at a few straws. If we spend the next two years playing with these programs, someone is going to, as they say in the management books, eat our lunch. Plus our benefactors have a fairly limited sense of humor about productivity. We simply must have results, not more promises."

He rocked back in his chair, thinking for a few minutes, then leaned forward toward the intercom next to his phone. He hesitated before he spoke to his secretary. "You have an extra hour or so?" Barbara nodded the affirmative.

"Annie," J. Cleveland McKeever said to his secretary. "Could you round up the members of our project teams and ask them to meet me here for about an hour?"

The group that filed in fifteen minutes later looked, Barbara thought, gloomy enough to be attending their own funerals. Jason Rice, head of the quality team, had hastily retied his tie, obviously with little success. He still wore a "Zero Defects!" button on his lapel. Teresa Ann Townsend looked cool enough in her charcoal gray suit, but she clutched her black leather briefcase so tightly that her knuckles were white with the effort. Sam Medley was the last person through the door, and, as usual, he was carrying a stack of computer printouts clutched to his chest like a newborn babe. A couple of sheets of the computer paper trailed behind him, flapping lightly.

"Good news, chief," Jason Rice said. "Our quality program is starting to show some hard results. Our roving inspectors picked up three percent fewer defects in this five-day period than in the last five-day period."

Barbara winced. The "roving inspectors" were all college students or recent grads with no shop floor experience at all and an attitude to match. Two of the lathe operators had suggested to Barbara that she recommend a couple of the roving inspectors be burned at the stake as a warning to the rest. Even Laura Meyers had few kind words for what she called "The Quality Police."

"It's just like being back in elementary school," Laura told Barbara bitterly. "Somebody gets singled out and made an example of. It just does wonders for morale. *Forget* quality!"

In the meeting, everyone waited with varying stages of impatience for some kind of response to Jason Rice's opening.

"I'm glad to hear it," J. Cleveland McKeever finally said. "Results are always good."

Sam Medley shuffled uncomfortably. He'd been there the longest, and the MRP II program was still stumbling. J.J. Jones had told Barbara that MRP II allowed them to "launch more orders with the speed of light and yet, amazingly, still keep the schedules wrong." Sam Medley no longer talked about "Class A" MRP II in 12 months.

"Results are what this little impromptu meeting is about," said J. Cleveland McKeever. "Barbara here has some interesting observations that I'd like her to share with the rest of you."

"The rest of you" shifted uncomfortably in their seats, except for Jason Rice, the eternal techie. He grinned at Barbara. Barbara figured he'd jump at a chance to move into CIM.

"We're talking major caliber mainframe here, aren't we?" he asked, practically rubbing his hands together in anticipation.

"Not exactly," Barbara replied, looking toward The Man, who picked up the ball.

"Barbara has some concerns that our problems stem more from business practices than a lack of computer hardware and software," J. Cleveland McKeever said, once again giving the floor back to Barbara, who briefly recapped her earlier discussion. She was met with three looks somewhere between outright skepticism and befuddlement.

"Before we go on, I'd like to add one other point," J. Cleveland said. "I received word in the last couple of days from the gnomes last week that we can expect some more competition very soon. In fact, my sources tell me that a Korean plant will be on line in less than six months. A fully automated, state-of-the-art Korean plant designed to produce plastic parts not only for their own industries, but in the open marketplace as well."

He had no need to pause for effect. Barbara was

stunned, and it was clear that the other project leaders were as well. For years T&P had held their market share not based on their efficiency and quality, but on the fact that they were there first with the necessary high-tech plastics. In fact, Barbara had found that many of the second-floor managers didn't even understand the need for becoming more efficient or more competitive, an attitude that was common even on the shop floor.

She spent more than one occasion with Red Dunn fencing over the issue of "competitiveness."

"Competitiveness is just another management word," he'd told her. "Look, we've been running the business this way for a long time. We make a profit. In a year or so there'll be another management word. We'll still be doing the same thing. All this company lacks is discipline. If everyone in the company cooperated, we wouldn't need all these words."

Dunn was echoed by Carl Layton in Accounting. "We make money, Barbara. And that's what this thing is all about, isn't it? We turn a steady four or five percent a year. We've held the same market share within a couple of points for the last ten years. We're *comfortable* here. What's the problem?"

The problem, Barbara thought wryly, had suddenly become self-evident.

"I'm afraid that's not all the bad news, either," The Man continued. "The gnomes tell me that by the end of the next calendar year, there'll be three more automated factories on-line in the Pacific Rim--at least one apparently bankrolled by China. Apparently somebody over there thinks our business would be a good business to get into in a big way."

J. Cleveland McKeever sat back in his upholstered chair and smiled his mild smile, but Barbara thought he looked very tired. It was easy to forget when you were down in the trenches that not all the corporate battles were fought on the shop floor; unfortunately, it also worked the opposite way.

"What I need from all of you now," he continued, "is a way we can compete in a world market. I don't see wholesale automation as a viable alternative"--he laughed again, with a nod toward Barbara--"I don't think we'll 'Automate Or Evaporate.' For a start, it costs too much. And, on a more personal level, we fought to keep T&P relatively independent in the buyout; I didn't go through that fight to replace half our employees with robots. But, and let me emphasize this point, I need a solution, and I need it soon."

"We already *have* a solution," said Teresa Ann Townsend. "We can move to a Just-In-Time environment tomorrow and realize enough savings to keep us on the playing field."

"The same goes for quality," said Jason Rice. "If we keep cracking down, we can keep our quality on par with even the newest automated plant."

Sam Medley didn't say anything at first, then couldn't help himself. "If we had gotten to 'Class A' on schedule, we wouldn't be in this fix..."

He stopped short.

"And we were going to do that in, what, eight months? One year? That didn't happen, did it? So you don't have an MRP II solution for me after all?" J. Cleveland McKeever asked. Sam Medley shook his head, then he looked at Barbara and smiled. *My first convert*, she thought, *and not a minute too soon.*

"Good," said J. Cleveland McKeever, "because we don't need a JIT solution, a Total Quality solution or an MRP II solution. We just need a solution--*results*--and we need them very quickly."

And with that, the meeting was over.

Chapter Six

Winds Of Change

Y ou know what I mean," the big man said. "You get up in the morning and it's colder than a well digger's, uh, hands." That got an appreciative chuckle, and Barbara was surprised that anybody could still laugh. "Your car won't start, right? Ain't nothing serious--you just need to hook up your cold battery to a warm one and jump it off. Starts right up. Well, folks, I think our battery's gone cold."

Cold hell, Barbara thought to herself. The thing's dead as a brick.

"I think J. Cleveland is right--we need some kind of a jumpstart," said Sam Medley. His jacket was off and the sleeves of his pink shirt were rolled up to his elbows. It was late afternoon, and the ten executives in the closed conference room had been meeting since 8:30 in the morning with breaks for only the most urgent caffeine or nicotine longings. All ten looked like they'd been vacationing in a sauna.

"Jumpstart?" someone said.

"More like, 'Jump ship,'" someone else murmured.

"What we've been meeting here to decide is which program we concentrate on implementing first," Medley continues. "We're all agreed that we can't do MRP II, JIT and TQC at the same time, right?"

About three of the people, including Barbara, nodded. Alyse Anderson from Purchasing continued using her mechanical pencil to flip paper clips into a nearby overflowing ashtray. Sam Medley took this to mean he had a general consensus and continued on.

"The real problem is which do we do first? I mean, I've been working on MRP II for almost two years now, and I'd sure like to see it finished..."

"So would we," said Alyse Anderson, flipping another paper clip. "More than you can ever imagine."

"...But I understand how Jason feels with his quality program..."

"Quality is what's going to make the difference," Jason Rice said with decorum.

"...And Teresa has been working like a dog getting the JIT stuff going..."

Teresa Ann Townsend nodded, and Barbara noticed that Teresa alone didn't look like she'd spent the day splashing around a heated pool in her business suit. How come, she wondered absently, that air conditioners never seem to work well in conference rooms?

Sam Medley started to stand. "...I say it's time we made a decision. I don't mean to sound partisan, but I say let's get MRP II going, get some kind of credibility in our schedules..."

"Here, here!" said Alyse. Red Dunn, his face red, scowled at the tall, gangly woman from purchasing. "If you could get the stuff here," he said, "we sure as hell could build it."

Alyse Anderson smiled sweetly. Sam Medley pressed on.

"...Then go straight into ramming home the quality program. As soon as we've got quality under control, *then* let's move to JIT with some work cells and some kanban cards and some set-up reduction stuff. That makes sense to me." With that, Sam Medley sat down. There was a scattering of applause, and a paperclip plopped into Sam's coffee cup.

Before Teresa Ann Townsend could stand to make her rebuttal or Jason Rice could finish frantically shuffling through a stack of computer paper, Barbara stood up, interrupting a conversation between a production engineer and Ann Rosetti from design engineering on bass fishing.

"I agree with Sam," Barbara said quickly, and

even the two engineers looked up. Through the interminable cycle of meetings that began when J. Cleveland McKeever threw out the bombshell on competition from the Pacific Rim, Barbara had emerged as the middle ground, the synthesis person. Which struck her as funny, since the only reason she held the middle ground was that she alone wasn't a partisan. "You sure you don't want to borrow a hat from the archives?" Laura Meyers had said when Barbara explained the meetings while the two women were working out the previous night. "How about a small gun?"

"We do need a jumpstart," Barbara continued. "But I don't think the jumpstart has to do with which program we implement first..."

"We implement CIM first, right?," said Jason Rice.

"Sem who?" asked Carl Layton from Accounting, which caused Jason Rice to color and the rest of the group to chuckle.

"All right," Barbara said. "Let's go back to the beginning. What are we trying to do here?"

"I don't know about the others," said Sam Medley, "but I'd like to see us reach 'Class A.'"

"So we're here to implement MRP II?" Barbara asked.

"Well, when you put it like that, no," replied Sam.

Before Sam could continue speaking, Alyse

Anderson from Purchasing paused from gathering her ammunition from across the tabletop and spoke.

"Survival," she said. "What we want to do here is figure out how to survive."

"She's right," said Teresa Ann Townsend. "What we're trying to do here is figure out a way to survive, and that means being competitive."

"More than that," added Fred Thomas from Sales. "What we want to do is more than survive, more than just run along in the race. We want to stone cold *win!*"

Red Dunn looked puzzled. "What you're saying," he said to the group, "is that if we don't beat the competition, or, I mean, win this race, we're going to be in trouble, right?"

"You could say trouble," said Fred Thomas. "I'd say unemployed."

"This isn't the first time a bunch of Suits cried wolf," Red Dunn said.

"That doesn't mean there aren't wolves out there this time," said Fred Thomas. "You start talking unemployment, and you've got my full attention. Some of my biggest customers are starting to hint about big-time price reductions to guarantee their continued purchases from us. They're starting to talk weekly, even *daily*, deliveries, all sorts of things. This is *real!*"

"But," said Jason Rice, "we can't win in a world

market without a quality program. It's that simple."

"But the quality program isn't the end," said Barbara, "just like JIT and MRP II aren't the end. They're just things we *have* to do to compete."

"What a novel idea," said Alyse Anderson going back to flipping paperclips. "But what does it mean?"

"I think it means," said Ann Rosetti from Engineering, who'd most recently been discussing bass fishing, "that we've taken our eyes off the ball. Heck, I haven't been paying that much attention, because I figure you guys can implement anything you want and it doesn't affect me all that much. We design the stuff, you know. We try not to get too bogged down in the day-to-day problems of the shop floor..."

Red Dunn huffed.

"I think I speak for all of Engineering, though, when I say losing our jobs affects us a whole bunch," Ann Rosetti said. "What you're saying is that we get better or we sink. Hang together or hang separately, right?"

Barbara nodded.

"Then how do we get better? How do we learn to play in a world class league?" the engineer continued. "Doesn't seem to me that it makes a whole heck of a lot of difference what we call the things we do to get better, just as long as we get better doing them."

Barbara said nothing, but her heart lurched. What the engineer was saying made more sense than anything else she'd heard--in fact, they were ideas she'd come up with on her own. When she'd voiced the ideas to Laura Meyers, the floor supervisor had been enthusiastic for the first time since Barbara had met her.

"It only makes sense," Laura had told her. "Sometimes it seems like those Suits on the second floor are like a bunch of car mechanics arguing about whether they should use a wrench, a screwdriver or a pair of pliers to repair a car. Not even mechanics, even--more like the guys who run the shop. *We're* the mechanics, and one day they tell us we can use the screwdrivers, then the next day we should use the pliers. Couple of weeks later we can get to the wrench. The car never gets fixed, and you've got a lot of unhappy mechanics down here."

"I played softball when I was a kid," said Ann Rosetti. "Heck, I still play softball! For a while we had A, B and C leagues. The girls were the Cs. My team was the best C team out there--we never lost, and it was comfortable. So I complained and complained and got us into B class, which was tougher. We played tough teams, and we won there, too. Each step up is tougher. Doesn't mean it's not worth doing."

"Amen," said Fred Thomas.

"That still doesn't answer the question of which program comes first, and I still vote for MRP II," said Sam Medley. He can't help being a Rambo, Barbara thought.

"Maybe we ought to do them all at the same time and see which one works best," said Red Dunn. "Hell, I guess that's what we're doing now, and it's not working worth a darn. My people get queasy whenever they see somebody coming toward them with a stack of computer printouts. And I've still got some questions."

"Let's try it this way," Ann Rosetti said. "I think we've gotten bogged down by seeing these new programs as package deals, you know, like those Europe-in-three-days tours. Air fare, transportation, meals, tips and lousy time included. Is that the way they really are, though? Teresa and I were sitting around talking one night about this stuff, and it didn't seem to me that you had to have work cells or kanban cards to get set-up time reductions. More like JIT was a set of tools, and you use the tool you need to fix the problem."

"Well, that makes sense," said Red Dunn. "That's what we've been saying all along on the shop floor. I got machines down there where the changeover is so long and so complicated that sometimes it gets screwed up, and we make bad parts. If we got that set-up hammered out a little, I'd bet we start seeing better quality, too."

"It *is* all tied together," Barbara said. "We do need integration, but not just *hardware* and *software* integration. We need to integrate *all* our tools if we're going to solve our problems."

The meeting went on for another hour, more animated than it had been in days, until Barbara called things to a halt.

"Anybody interested in going home?" she said and immediately was the recipient of a standing ovation. "Okay, okay. So we're agreed that our goal, our mission, if you will, is to become a world class competitor, not to implement any one specific acronym?"

Again, applause.

"Let's pick it up from there tomorrow," she said, packing up her own papers and heading for the door.

She took a swing by the MIS department before she left and found Fast Eddie sipping his twenty-fifth Diet Coke of the day, doodling on the keyboard of his own aging portable computer. He listened with interest to her recounting of the day's meeting, then wrinkled his brows.

"I'll bet you get some problems that you haven't seen coming yet," he said.

"I'm game," Barbara said. "Let's hear 'em."

"Okay, so you've got a consensus that the goal

is world class, right?"

Barbara agreed.

"You also got a bunch of people hired to implement specific programs," Fast Eddie continued. "Are they going to wake up 'long about two a.m. this morning and say, 'Wait a minute! What just happened to my job?'"

Barbara laughed.

"I know it's not funny, Eddie," she said. "But I can't think about that just yet. I'm still trying to figure out where to connect the battery cables for that jumpstart."

"Maybe I can help," Fast Eddie said, shutting down his own computer. "Meanwhile, if I'm not sadly mistaken, it's beer-thirty."

Chapter Seven

The Turnaround

Fast Eddie Murdock's contribution came from a totally unexpected direction.

"I've been thinking about what you said about education," Fast Eddie told her the next morning. "How maybe a lot of our problems were coming from our education program--actually, our lack of education program. I remember I got stuck going to a Saturday seminar on 'Integrating The PC Into A Mainframe Environment: A Radical Approach.' Along about the middle of the afternoon, I was looking out the window at how nice it was and getting madder and madder..."

Barbara laughed. "Yeah, it's like being kept after school, isn't it?"

"...And I didn't learn anything," he continued. "That's another problem with education. Bad word. Something you do while you're in a class, shoved down your throat. And learning is not what we're talking about, I think. That's a part of it, sure--you can't use the tools if you don't know which end does what. But I think what we're really talking about is changing the way our people think, sort of changing the way they approach their jobs. We've all been off here on tangents--heck, I'm as guilty as the next guy. You can't run an MIS department without having a little bitty fascination with hardware..."--he laughed, falling easily back into his good ole boy routine--"...But you've done a good job of getting us cranked around to the idea of one game plan. Heck, I think even old Red Dunn half thinks you're on the right track. So the problem I see now is how do we learn to use the tools."

Fast Eddie began booting up his portable computer, and pretty soon the amber screen glowed. With a few keystrokes, he called up another program, then motioned Barbara to join him.

"Since you started talking about education," he began, "I decided to help things out by creating a little data base on what kind of outside education was available. Least, I thought it was going to be a little data base! Whew! There's everybody out there except Classes-R-Us, and I figure that's because nobody's thought of it yet. Look here..."

Barbara peered over Fast Eddie's shoulder. Only Eddie, she thought, would take the trouble to create such an elegant screen for a nickel-and-dime database. She reached over his shoulder and began scrolling through the various classes available. Eddie wasn't kidding, she mused, there were tons of them.

"Let's see, you got your cheerleaders..."

"What are they?" Barbara asked.

"Big name guys who come in and pump everybody up, maybe do one or two giant classes for a few hundred people," Fast Eddie replied. "We tried that for the jitterbugs, I think. Or maybe it was quality. Works for about an hour after they leave. Anyway, then you got your specialists. Some consultants got course catalogs like telephone books. We tried that, too, sending a few people here, a few people there, MRP II, JIT, see where that got us. Trapped in smorgasbord education."

Dueling project teams, Barbara agreed mentally.

"My personal favorites are the video courses," Fast Eddie continued, scrolling to another section of the file. "I guess they do a good job of getting the basics across, but, good lord, are they dull! I'd as soon as watch paint dry."

"Don't we have a boxful of one of those 'talking heads' video courses around here somewhere?" Barbara asked.

"Couple of 'em," he said. "They like to show us about two hours worth of videos, then let us have an *intensive* 15-minute discussion period. I think they got that sequence badly reversed. We need to be watching a little and talking *a lot!* By the way, check out my personal favorite video, the one on MRP II. Volume Eight, to be exact."

"Why?"

"'Cause Allison took Volume Eight home and fixed it up," he said cryptically. "If you're a big fan of Arnold Schwarzenegger, it could be the best MRP II video you'll ever see. She edited all the fight scenes from his last three movies into about ten minutes. The video is like 'Conan the Barbarian meets the MRP II Gurus'."

Barbara laughed and continued scrolling back and forth through the file.

"So what do you think?" Fast Eddie said.

"Integrators," Barbara said abruptly. "We need the opposite of people with individual classes on each subject. We need people who want to show us how all these techniques work together--assuming, of course, the darn things work together at all."

"Well, that's a much shorter list," Fast Eddie said, tweaking the computer again.

"You know, the more I think about it, the more I think we need the people who've been into integration from the beginning, not just the Jilly-Come-Latelys..."

"Jilly?"

"It's a new world, Eddie," Barbara said. "So

find us the first and the best."

"No problem," he said.

A couple of hours later she walked out of J. Cleveland McKeever's office with a commitment to send several critical people to a comprehensive class Fast Eddie had ferreted out. It didn't come without a short battle.

"Barbara, I know you mean well, but $25,000 is a lot of money already committed to education," he had said.

Barbara, though, had done her homework. There were two crucial points. The first was that the dueling acronyms had to end before any progress could be made.

"We're not trying to implement an acronym," she told her boss. "We trying to become a world class competitor. That means using the correct tool to solve the problem at hand. And we need some help in how to do that. We don't need a class in how to implement JIT or how to become a 'Class A' MRP II company or the path to TQC. We need a class in how to use those tools to solve our problems. We can have meetings and run around in circles for another couple of years and still be no closer to world class than we are now."

The other critical point, she'd continued, was the concept of education itself. The most progressive companies in the world, she'd discovered, companies who weren't afraid to go one-on-one in a tough world market, were scaling up their education budgets.

"It's the word *education* we're stumbling on," she'd told the CEO of T&P. "We don't really mean education, like classrooms and books and pop quizzes. But as soon as we say the word, that's what pops into peoples' heads. What we're really talking about is people doing their jobs differently, changing the way our people do business. And that's not just the shop floor. If we could get Sales and Manufacturing talking to one another, think of the potential!"

The Man nodded his head in agreement.

"But then we make it worse by *acting* like we're back in school, dragging people out on their days off or after work and making them suffer through boring lectures or endless *videos!*"

"Did you happen to see the MRP II video?" J. Cleveland McKeever asked, smiling. "Volume Eight was my favorite."

"We don't need classroom lectures and pop quizzes," Barbara pressed on. "We need to let our people *talk*. They've got problems with what we're doing. Sometimes, they don't understand how critical it is that we make ourselves into world class competitors. I mean, they've heard this song before. They want to know how our plans affect their jobs, their work days, their pensions, their benefits, their job security. And the heck of it is, half the time, we can't tell 'em, because we don't know ourselves. We need help."

"And how, exactly, will more classes help us?" J. Cleveland McKeever asked, templing his hands in the familiar gesture of thought.

"We need integrators. People who can show us how MRP II, JIT, TQC, heck, maybe CIM and any of those other acronyms lying around fit together," Barbara said. "We've got good people, but they're pulling against each other. It's taken us the better part of two months just to reach an agreement on the fact that the mission is excellence, not implementing an acronym. But that single focus is fragile right now--I'd like to see us get a general overview of what we need to do, so we'll have a common understanding. We need hard facts and hard techniques to make that single focus real. We need to get away from the company as a group and mix with people from other companies--try to get an objective view. Half of getting rid of that 'we're unique' viewpoint is meeting other people with the same problems. I think that's the only way we're going to get the facts and techniques we need. It also doesn't hurt to meet with people from other companies going through the same things we are. We need *that*.

"Don't get me wrong," she added quickly. "I

don't think going to classes is the entire answer. But it's a catalyst to get the process going, to get the results you want. It's a start, but an important start."

"What about bringing a consultant here to teach?" he asked.

"It didn't work before. Why should it work now?" she said. "Besides, from my own experience, it's easier to learn outside of the everyday work environment. Good grief, just to get away from the constant interruptions and distractions gives us a little edge. And we need every edge we can get. We need to spread I guess you'd call it the ownership of the new programs throughout the company, and I don't think we can do that in a hit-and-run manner."

J. Cleveland McKeever nodded.

"About the expense..."

Before he could finish his sentence, Barbara was off and running again.

"I was hired to figure out a way to tie all this hardware and software together, buy whatever was necessary to do the job. What are we talking there--two mil, three mil? And nobody even flinches. At every company I've worked in, someone has always said, 'Well, if that's what it takes to win, let's do it.'" she said. "But when we talk about investing in our people, our most important resource, a lot of people look at the floor. Did you know Motorola spends $44 million a year on employee education? They're tired of playing second fiddle to the Japanese!"

"Whoa! Okay, I'm sold. I'm sold," he said, and Barbara suspected he'd been sold for some time. *He just wanted to see me work*, she thought.

"Get me a plan this afternoon, and I'll approve it," The Man said.

"I'd like to start with sending ten people, myself included, to an overview class. This class isn't tied to a single acronym, and that's the way we have to go," she said, pulling out the plan she'd hastily worked out with Fast Eddie. "I'd like to start with myself, the three project team heads, Red Dunn, Laura Meyers, who I've been working with on the shop floor and representatives from Sales, Accounting, Purchasing and Engineering."

"Why someone from the floor so early?" he asked.

"Because she had a great line the other day," Barbara replied. "She said, 'You know, Barbara, that you can't shove this stuff down our throats. Change doesn't come from the top down; it comes from the bottom up.' I think she's right, and I think we need her help."

"Classes again," J. Cleveland McKeever sighed. "Why do I suspect that the next thing I know you'll be sending me to class?"

Chapter Eight

Momentum

Teresa Ann Townsend was bubbling over with enthusiasm, a sight which Barbara found fairly amusing. For most of the time Barbara had been at TeePee, Teresa Ann Townsend had barely cracked a smile, much less get excited. Now she had her gray pin-striped jacket off two hours into a meeting with Sam Medley, three engineers and a couple of representatives from the shop floor, including Laura Meyers. The topic of the meeting was "How Are We Going To Run The Business Differently?," one of dozens of such meetings going on throughout the company.

And it made sense, Barbara thought. The classes had confirmed Laura Meyers' gut-level feelings that change couldn't be shoved down people's throats from on high. Instead, change came from the bottom up.

"And how," one of the instructors had intoned, "do we get change from the bottom up? How do we find out what the problems and the fears and the concerns of the people throughout the plant are? Well, here's a pretty scientific method--we ask them."

That had gotten a good laugh in the class. But it was an uncomfortable laugh--Barbara knew that surprisingly few managers had actually taken the time to ask their people what the problems were. And even that made sense. As industry had heated up, become more global and more competitive, the amount of work seemed to multiply ten-fold. From Barbara's own experience, most of a manager's time seemed to be taken up in putting out fires rather than in running the business. And that was a key point from the classes.

But the whole issue of change, of behavioral modification, was tricky. If you, as Ann Rosetti from Engineering had put it before the classes even began, lost sight of the ball, started focusing on implementing a single acronym rather than bringing about the behavioral changes necessary for running the business differently, all the possible advantages seemed to evaporate into the mists--exactly what had happened at T&P.

"It's not a question of whether we implement MRP II or JIT or TQC," the instructor had said again and again. "What we have to do first is decide how we must run the business differently."

It was such a basic question that it caught everybody off-guard, but over the course of a week, everyone in the class began to see how all the various issues that seemed unrelated focused back to that same basic question.

For the people from T&P, the first thing that really brought it together was the question of bill of material accuracy. Record accuracy, Barbara knew, was considered a primary focus area for MRP II. If the planning system was going to work correctly, the bill of material--what was being used to make the product--had to be correct. Sam Medley had concentrated on getting the bills 75 percent accurate, and he was creeping up on 85 percent--and becoming more than just a little disillusioned.

"Nobody really gives a darn," Sam had confided to Barbara one afternoon. "Most of the lines work from their own little 'black books,' sort of personal bills of material, so it doesn't make that much difference whether the bills in the computer are accurate or not. Nobody really understands what the big deal is about."

On this particular day the instructor had described a method for relieving the inventory on lines where large amounts of the same items were made each day. The technique was called backflushing, and both Teresa Ann Townsend's and Laura Meyers' eyes lit up. It was the perfect way to handle not only Laura's line, but several of the other assembly lines at T&P. It took no imagination at all to see how much simpler life would be using such a system, plus it would move toward Teresa Ann's JIT ideal of "material comes in the morning; product is shipped in the afternoon."

"Damn!" said Red Dunn, who, up until that point had been studiously doodling on his notebook and trying not to be caught paying attention. "That would work great for us..."--then he realized he was still in class and flushed bright red.

"I mean, it would," he stammered to the chuckles of the class. "But doesn't that mean that the records have to be dead accurate or you're going to paint yourself into a corner mighty quickly?"

"That is," said the instructor, "exactly right." And Red Dunn shined with the extra attention. "If the records aren't accurate, you're in trouble so deep you'll never get out--your successor might, but you'd better have your resume updated."

"Now," the instructor had continued, "what are we talking about implementing here? MRP II? JIT? TQC?"

The class--especially the people from T&P--had gotten the point.

"How about 'None Of The Above' or 'All Of The

Above'? The fact is that we need record accuracy, which is associated with MRP II," continued the instructor. "We're also moving to a more flow environment, which we usually think of as a JIT issue. And don't forget that it's vitally important to satisfy the expectations of our 'customers'--in this case the customers are the downstream users of the parts we're making. If we don't produce quality parts for the next person on the line, we're going to see the flow environment start to break down. In fact, aren't record accuracy, valid schedules and integrated sales and operations plans all really quality issues. *Quality is conformance to expectations*. And we expect our schedules to be valid, we expect our records to be accurate, we expect our planning to be focused on a single goal."

The instructor added that, of course, we wanted to flatten the bill of material--a JIT goal--but that required we observe the manufacturing process to make sure the bill reflected that process, which got an "Ah hah!" from Laura Meyers and an embarrassed look from Sam Medley, recalling his ill-fated attempt to make the manufacturing process on Laura's line conform to an arbitrary bill.

In some ways the class was a revelation. The project teams had struggled for so long to implement a specific acronym that they had, in fact, lost sight of the forest. And it was a far too common problem. The people from Engineering and Purchasing and Accounting were pretty sure none of it applied to them anyway, and the shop floor didn't trust anybody.

The strength of the Japanese, the instructor had reminded the class, was that they understood the enemy--the competition--was *outside*, not *inside*, the company.

"We're all on the same team," the instructor said. "Sometimes we need to be reminded of that fact."

A large section of the class, to Barbara's relief, centered on how to get the whole team working together, how to get everyone to "buy into" the quest for world class.

"My biggest fear," Barbara had told Laura Meyers before leaving for the class, "is that they're going to tell us all this great stuff, and then not give us any way to make it work here."

"That would be about par," Laura said caustically. She was less-than-enthused with the whole plan.

"So you're all here being educated," the instructor had said. "We crack open your head and pour in some knowledge. Just like that. Does anybody out there have a problem with the word 'education'?"

Barbara was surprised to see about half the

room raise their hands. And everybody's problems were pretty much the same.

"What we're talking about is a change in culture, a behavioral change," the instructor told the class. "That's the only way these programs are going to work. That's a heck of a lot more than a couple of free donuts and a Saturday afternoon class."

"Sure, people need to learn how to use the tools," the instructor said. "But the bulk of what we like to call our business meetings--meetings to discuss the way we want to run the business differently--has to be *discussion.*"

People aren't afraid of change, the instructor had told the class, but they are afraid of the unknown.

"We have this tremendous resource in our people," he continued. "Our people, this Silent Majority of people, who neither help nor hinder, have the answers to the toughest questions we can throw at them. *They* can tell us how to run the business better, how to become world class competitors. All we have to do is have them on our side."

But the Silent Majority, the 90 percent of the people who are neither for nor against the new programs, have specific fears and uncertainties. Will the new ideas work? How will the new programs impact on their jobs? Will they even still have a job? Is the management support really there, or is this just another fad? Do these radical new ideas really apply to their business at all? And, finally, is the result worth it, really worth it?

"Those are questions that have to be answered if we're going to swing the Silent Majority to our side," the instructor said. "And discussion is the way you answer people's questions, clear up their concerns and address their fears."

Instead of education, what will be needed is a series of meetings, small groups of people from different departments, discussing the way the business is to be run--call them *business meetings.*

"And those business meetings shouldn't be general gripe sessions," the instructor continued. "Each meeting should focus on a particular topic, say reducing lead times. Use the first ten to fifteen minutes of the meeting to learn why shorter lead times are better. There's where your videos might come in. The next hour, though, is *discussion,* centered on how to overcome the obstacles to reducing lead times. See why it's necessary to have all areas of the company represented here? The obstacles might come from anywhere. The long lead time might come from set-up problems, or it might come from problems with the vendors. As we plan to attack the problem, we're starting to build the invaluable commodity of teamwork. People are making real changes, and they're working together to do it. Interdepartmental barriers come down. Communications open up. Does any of this sound good to you guys?"

Alyse Anderson laughed. "I wouldn't know what to say if Engineering talked to me," she said.

"Figures," said Ann Rosetti wryly. "That's why we never talked to you before."

"The way I see it," Red Dunn said, "is we've got to concentrate on how we can apply the ideas we've learned and figure out how to overcome whatever obstacles we run into. That's going to take everyone in the company being involved. It's a big job."

Chapter Nine

Meeting The Challenge

At T&P, the business meetings faced a rocky road in the beginning--the general consensus, especially on the shop floor, was "Scam."

"The least they could have done was give us baseball caps," grumbled one drill press operator. As the meetings progressed, though, as predicted, the barriers began breaking down. Barbara sat in on one particular meeting where a local woman who'd been working the same machine since the plant opened dragged Jason Rice over the coals for the "Quality Police." Her work station was surrounded with pictures of her grandchildren, small framed quilt squares and even an African violet. Barbara suspected it looked exactly like the woman's living room at home.

"You think I don't have sense enough to build a TPAA662 without some smart-mouth kid standing over my shoulder?" the grandmotherly woman had asked the embarrassed younger man, who quickly started explaining about modern electronic test equipment and digital micrometers and the like. Before he could get too carried away, she interrupted him.

"Sonny," the older woman had said, "One of my grandmother's quilts hangs in a museum on down in Nashville. When they hung that quilt, they decided to measure the number of stitches, for whatever reason they do things like that. What they found, young man, was 100 stitches per inch. Not 101 stitches. Not 99 stitches. Exactly 100 stitches per inch. By hand. By kerosene lantern. And now you're telling me that her daughter's daughter doesn't have sense enough to push a button and read a meter? What I do, young man, I do *right*. If you can tell me what you want, I can make it, and make it right."

She got an ovation from the other members of the group, and Barbara felt a swelling of pride herself. *They want to do good work,* she thought. *They want to win. We all want to win. This is going to work...*

"Quality at the source," a flustered Jason Rice answered.

"Darn right," the drill press operator said. "You tell us what you want, and you give us the tools, and by gosh, we'll make what you need, and we'll make it right the first time."

Each business meeting had centered on a

specific topic, such as vendor partnerships or set-up reduction or record accuracy. In the begin-ning, the core group of people who had attended the outside classes served as leaders of the busi-ness meetings. The first thirty minutes or so of the two-hour meetings were dedicated to learn-ing the concepts--the tools--for change. One of the biggest stumbling blocks initially was seman-tics. Each acronym area, even each department of the company, had its own specialized vocabulary, and one of the important first steps was to make sure that everyone was speaking the same language. If a videotape applied to the topic at hand, it was shown in the early part of the meeting. The rest of the meeting was discussion aimed at the topic at hand. Barbara was amazed how quickly everyone involved got over the "bitch session" mentality and got down to work. It was as if there was a huge amount of creative energy just waiting to get loose, to solve the problems facing T&P, and the company had final-ly found a way to tap those human resources.

One of the biggest surprises was Red Dunn, who had gone from skeptic to supporter. He'd main-tained his skepticism until the business meeting on vendor partnerships, which included Alyse Anderson and her assistant from Purchasing, a couple of Planning and Scheduling people, two representatives from Sales and one of Jason

Rice's QA people. The meeting also included J.J. Jones, one of the foremost proponents of the "nuke them before they nuke us" vendor policy, which, as Red Dunn stated for the record, was a lot closer to his own personal opinions than any newfangled idea of vendor partnerships.

"You can't form partnerships with thieves," said J.J., and Red nodded his head approvingly.

When the discussion began, though, an interesting point started to surface. In several cases T&P's needs had changed, but nobody had informed the vendors; they were delivering to specs in some cases ten years out of date. Red held the meeting up until a couple of engineers, including Ann Rosetti, could be rounded up to participate.

In the meantime, the team tackled lot sizes.

"Why do we order plastic beads in such large lot sizes?" J.J. Jones asked one of the Purchasing people.

"Price break," Alyse Anderson responded, almost reflexively. "Amounts to about a four percent break."

J.J. nodded, but Red latched onto the figure.

"Wonder how much it costs us to store the stuff," he said, pulling out his calculator and doing some figuring.

"The vendors like to deliver in those lot sizes," Alyse added. "At least, that's what they've always delivered in."

"It costs the same to store the stuff as the price break," Red Dunn announced. "There's really no break at all."

"What about the quality problems with the incoming material?" asked the QA rep. "The beads have to be within a certain tolerance to feed through our automatic machinery. We sample each batch, and we've rejected five, maybe six percent for the beads being too large."

"That's interesting," Ann Rosetti said, walking into the room. "That's what we specified. I checked before I came, and the specs are seven years old. You know, we upgraded our machinery about three years ago, and the new stuff is a lot more sensitive to bead size than the old machines. I wonder if we updated our specs for the vendor?"

"We don't talk to each other," Red Dunn said wryly. "What makes you think we talked to the vendor? I mean, heck, he's in another town!"

As the meeting progressed, everyone began to see that not only was there a communication problem, but that the solutions cut across the various acronyms. Smaller lot sizes were thought of as a JIT issue. But in order to get those smaller lot sizes, which Red Dunn claimed would simplify his capacity problems, the vendors would have to make more frequent deliveries, and that would require a valid schedule, which was typically an

MRP II bailiwick. And for frequent deliveries of small quantities not to shut the plant down, the quality of the incoming material had to be high, a TQC issue.

Red Dunn came out of that meeting convinced that at least some of the problems were solvable--and not by throwing money or computer chips at them.

One of the most interesting early business meetings, Barbara thought, was the one on Sales and Operations Planning, the idea of creating one game plan for the entire company. It started out like a cross between a Chinese fire drill and World War III. Sales opened fire on Engineering for delaying the special promotion fire truck. Purchasing fired a few shots at Sales. Sales got ready to retaliate, but before the shots could be fired, J. Cleveland McKeever, who'd dropped by the meeting held up his hand for peace and made an announcement.

"This meeting has convinced me that Barbara Pilot was right; we were wrong about education. In fact, listening to you all talk has convinced me that I don't know enough about integrating the new programs," The Man said. "So I'll be going to outside classes myself, as well as my Vice Presidents and the department heads who haven't already been. When we get back, we'll start our own business meetings every Tuesday morning to discuss how these concepts change our jobs. I think that will help."

That gave everyone in the meeting pause. If the programs were so important that the CEO of the company was going back to school, then maybe there had better be less finger pointing and more discussion.

Each business meeting led to more business meetings, branching off into more and more topics. Barbara told Laura Meyers that the best thing about the meetings was, "results."

"People can really see things happen," she said. "They can see changes, not just talk about changes."

Even the role of the computer, of software and automation, began to make more sense.

"It's easy enough," Alyse Anderson said. "We use the computer to recalculate the new requirements for purchased material when the schedule changes. Quickly. Then we can communicate the new info to our vendors."

"Heck, maybe they could get the stuff here on time then," J.J. Jones said mischievously.

"The new software package," Fast Eddie Murdock added, "is going to help us integrate all that disconnected Purchasing, inventory control and Accounting systems a little better. Who knows-- maybe the whole place will start running on time..."

"Just tools," Red Dunn said one day. "Software upgrades. New computers. Automation. All just tools. And darn if they don't look like pretty valuable tools at that."

The purpose of the business meetings was to sway what the original group of people had started referring to as the Core Group, a portion of the Silent Majority. The Core Group was composed of the opinion leaders--"Troublemakers," Laura Meyers had sniffed. "Like you?" Barbara had pointed out--people who were influential or just listened to by other people. If the Core Group, opinion leaders from all departments-- people like J.J. Jones and Red Dunn and Fred Thomas and Carl Layton--could be won over, then eventually, the entire Silent Majority would follow.

One of the turning points was clearly the trip to a special executive class by J. Cleveland Mc-Keever and the top management of T&P.

"They put their money where their mouth was," Fast Eddie Murdock said. "I'll be damned."

Chapter Ten

The Race Under Way

Floyd the Fixer led Barbara through the maze of older buildings and additions that made up T&P, all the way back to the earliest section of the plant, where twenty or so people assembled red fire trucks. Actually, as the fire trucks became a smaller and smaller part of T&P's output, the fire truck line kept shrinking, until the original space was used as much for storage as for assembly of the toys. Still, everybody knew J. Cleveland McKeever loved the red trucks, and, Barbara had discovered, to her surprise, the darn things were actually a profitable item.

Barbara had worried that Floyd would be one of the hardest sells on the new programs. After all, he'd been there decades, and he'd seen the various management fads and super computer programs come and go. "Like missiles," he'd said. "Blast up, fall down." Barbara suspected he was a closet contributor to Laura's archives. Floyd, though, had surprised everyone. He practically dove into the business meetings, devouring huge chunks of the new techniques in a single sitting. His questions were thoughtful, timely and often helped some of the shier employees articulate their own concerns.

One day Barbara caught him bustling around the shop floor.

"You seem pretty pleased about the way things are going," she said.

"Ah," replied the Fixer. "What you mean is you're surprised that I'm not more upset that my job is disappearing."

Barbara punched him on the shoulder. "It's getting so you can't sneak anything past anybody these days," she said.

"Let me tell you," he said, puffing his way along the shop floor like an animated beach ball. "I came here years ago from another factory in town, got laid off when a company in Kentucky slipped in and took the market away from the people I worked for. We all saw it comin', but nobody thought to ask us about anything. Heck, now every time I turn around, somebody's asking me what I think, or what I can do to make things better. And, boy, I'll tell you. I got ideas backed up for 20 years."

"You're not worried about your job?" she asked, although she knew the answer.

"J. Cleveland says nobody loses their job because of productivity increases," Floyd said. "I ain't sayin' I haven't heard that before, but, you know, actions speak a whole bunch louder than words. Blending's got a head start on us, and it looked like they were going to idle about five guys with things running smoother. I just mentioned that it might be nice to have some people crossed-trained on several machines, 'case we got an illness or something, and the next thing I know, we got guys from Blending training on drill presses, sanders, buffers and lathes."

"What's the union think?"

"Down here, unions think what the members think," Floyd said. "The members think that cross-training might be a good way to protect your job when things get tough. The more you can do, the harder it is to do without you. Besides, it's fun to move around, not get stuck pushing the same button for 20 years or so."

Barbara also knew that Floyd had been huddled with the Engineering Department, looking at designs for new products and making suggestions on how those products might be made more "manufacturable." That was one of the side effects of the barriers coming down. Months had passed since the first business meetings began. For the first time, Engineering and the shop floor were discussing how to build stuff without pointing fingers and shouting at each other. Engineers actually walked from their office to the shop floor to ask questions, and it wasn't unusual to see a floor supervisor spending lunch with the engineers, pouring over drawings.

The most important thing, Barbara thought, was the feeling, the sense that people were actually working together toward a common goal, the mission of becoming world class.

As predicted, the Korean plant had come online, and T&P quickly lost two old and valued customers. That sent shock waves to the parent company, who turned those shock waves around and aimed them at Kingsport. The message was clear--*let's see some results, and let's see them quickly*.

"It's one hell of a problem," said Fast Eddie Murdock. "We get backed into a corner, and somebody starts screaming do something, even if it's wrong. Next thing you know, people are going to be screaming to buy a new computer and automate everything."

Fast Eddie smirked.

"It's a valid point," Barbara said, ignoring the jab. "Speaking as a former academic, we've had some good years of productivity increases by doing the obvious big things--closing down unprofitable plants, modernizing our factories, mergers, stuff like that. Big problems, you know. And you get in the mode of solving those big multimillion dollar problems. The last thing a busy executive wants to hear is that instead of one big $20 million problem, there's a million $20 problems to be solved."

"Yeah," Fast Eddie said. "You can't cowboy all those little problems. It takes the whole team hammering way at them, all the time."

"'Continuous improvement', as our friends across the Pacific say."

"I'm just thankful we don't have to do calisthenics in the morning," Fast Eddie continued. "Or wear those little company jumpsuits that'd make us look like attendants in an all-night car wash. Or sing the company anthem..."

"I wrote a company anthem," chimed in Allison from across the room. "Does anybody want to hear it? It's to the tune of 'Bad To The Bone.'"

The entire MIS department gave her a rousing "No!," sending the young computer programmer back to work designing a reporting system for overhead absorption that was not based on making as much as you can--a crash project for both MIS and Accounting.

"At least we're definitely hammering away," said Barbara. "We've just got to be careful not to lose sight of the ball. We have to remember the Mission--world class--to win the competitive race."

Floyd was proud as a new papa of the fire truck

line, which had become the test for some of the ideas and techniques being filtered into the rest of the plant. The most recent changes, which had been worked out between Teresa Ann Townsend, Sam Medley and a team of line workers, changed the fire truck assembly line into work cells, one making the chassis, the other assembling the body parts, a third creating the final product.

The first thing Barbara noticed was an absence of piles of materials next to each machine. The lot sizes had gotten smaller and smaller, and the work-in-process had shrunk as the fire truck line moved toward a JIT environment. And even with less inventory, they'd gone six weeks in a row with no shortages. The vendors had turned out not to have fangs. In fact, once T&P started talking to their vendors, they'd discovered that the frustration had worked both ways.

"Heck," J.J. Jones told Barbara. "If they'd known what we wanted, they'd have given it to us. I guess nobody can read minds."

"You know," Teresa Ann Townsend said to Barbara at a recent meeting. "The hardest thing for me to realize was that all that work-in-process was a security blanket for the people running the machines. Here I was telling them to shrink the lot size, and what they *heard* was me trying to shrink them right out of existence."

The younger woman had just shaken her head.

"That's a lesson I learned," she said.

Now the fire truck line moved like lightning, able to turn out fire trucks almost twice as fast as before.

"And if we make all the fire trucks we need," Floyd said proudly, "we shut down the line, and I move the people over to where they are needed. In fact, 90 percent of the people on the fire truck line are cross-trained on three or more machines."

Barbara recognized a couple of the machine operators as former members of Jason Rice's quality shock troops, recently disbanded.

"They turned out to be pretty nice kids once they got over being policemen," Floyd said. "And you know what else? Quality is way up."

The meeting in J. Cleveland McKeever's office was substantially different than other previous meetings Barbara remembered. For a start, no one appeared to be shellshocked--tired, maybe, but a *good* tired--and the news at the weekly upper management meeting was, if not good, then better.

"We lost almost nine percent of our market share to foreign competition within six months," J. Cleveland McKeever was saying, "but it looks like we've got the slide stopped. In fact"--he looked around the room significantly--"it looks like we're going to pick up a couple of our old clients. Amazingly, we are clobbering the competition on delivery time while holding the line on price. I'm really looking forward to taking this quarter's earnings report to corporate."

To Barbara, that was the true sign the new programs--the new culture--was starting to take hold. On-time delivery, a long-time bugaboo at T&P, had sort of taken on a life of its own. On-time delivery was a part of quality, just like building a product that worked, and the people on the floor took justifiable pride as their on-time deliveries, as charted on a huge wall-sized piece of cardboard erected by the line workers themselves, crept up on 80 percent. Barbara also knew that the relationship between the Engineering Department and floor supervisors such as Floyd had started paying dividends--the last few engineering change notices she'd seen were aimed at making some of the older products easier to manufacture.

When J. Cleveland McKeever came back from the top management class, he made a point of attending some of the executive business meetings himself, and that sent an undeniable message to everyone from vice president down to the newest janitor. Laura Meyers summed it up best, Barbara thought, when she told a meeting of her own people that, "This time, it's for real."

One of the first things The Man did was tackle the Sales, Manufacturing, Engineering and Finance communication problem. "I intend," he told Barbara, "to never have anyone surprise me with horror stories about orange fire trucks again! From now on, everyone knows what's going on, and we're going to have numbers that can be carved in stone. We are meeting every month without fail. In fact, I *personally* wrote the Sales and Operation Planning Policy."

Barbara had even gone down to a local sporting goods store and had a baseball cap custom made for the archives--"World Class" was the simple logo above a picture of a red fire truck. They'd ended up making a run of the hats; this time by popular demand.

The heads of the three project teams had formed a defacto project team of their own, charged by The Man himself with, "What's next?" The new project team worked with each department, targeting rough areas and working with the people in the department to smooth those areas out.

"We are, I think, coming up on a very dangerous time," J. Cleveland McKeever told his weekly meeting. Earlier, Barbara had come by his office and found him uncharacteristically staring out the window. "If I'd only been paying more attention," he'd said. "If myself and the other top management had been the first to go to those classes instead of the last, maybe we could have headed some of this off, not had these projects floundering for so long. We could have had results much sooner--and cheaper. Maybe we wouldn't be playing catch-up."

Barbara found herself moved.

"At least," she'd said, "we're playing some mighty tough catch-up." The Man had laughed.

"We have come very far," J. Cleveland Mc-Keever told the people around the conference table. "And we've achieved some important goals. The tendency, I think, is to sit back and rest on our laurels. Which is, of course, exactly how we got into the bad situation in the first place. Had we done what we finally did, go to the classes first to give us the proper perspective, integrated instead of trying to push through acronyms, get everyone involved, to buy in, we would now be at the head of the race. Many of the problems we blamed on software and hardware, we created ourselves.

"My question, then," he continued, "is how do we institutionalize change?"

It was a question on everyone's mind--how to become the long distance runner rather than the sprinter. In a year, or five years, the competition was still going to be there, tougher than ever. How would we compete?

"Does anyone have any ideas?" J. Cleveland Mc-Keever asked.

"Continuous improvement," said Jason Rice. "It's a hard thing to realize that what we're talking about is a journey, not a destination. Kind of grinds against our upbringing a little. But it's true. We've got to keep the lines of communication open and keep making those little changes."

"I have an idea, too," said Teresa Ann Townsend. "Trust our people. Listen to them. Get them involved. They've got the answers, if we just give them the tools."

She couldn't, thought Barbara, be any more right.

FINIS

The following two Appendices are excerpted from **Hot List II**, a quarterly newsletter from R.D. Garwood, Inc. For information on receiving **Hot List II** or ordering additional copies of Jumpstart, please see the order form following the Appendices.

World Class Performance: Going For The Gold

By Dave Garwood

Quality assurance is now a key marketing strategy," read the headline in a recent article in our local Atlanta newspaper.

What a breakthrough in competitive strategy! Make products that work, treat the customers well, and they'll come back and buy more. Heavy thinking!

The article went on to say "Manufacturers have been forced to improve quality to compete against foreign companies ..." What a shame. Do we have to be forced to give the customer quality? Maybe the prescription for winning a gold medal in the global Competitive Race isn't all that complex after all.

There's no question that the Competitive Race has been heating up, becoming more crowded every day. The competitors are getting leaner and meaner. The good news is that many companies are winning--bringing home the gold. For them, the issue is how to stay in front. For other companies, though, the issue is still how to get in front.

Who decides the winner of the Competitive Race?

The answer is obvious: The Customers choose! The gold medals are called purchase orders and contracts. The

World- Class Competetive Standards

	— OLD —	— NEW —
Quality	95-98% Yield	99.9999%
Inventory	2-6 Turns	20-50 Spins
Service	± 1 Week	Just-In-Time
Lead Times	Weeks	Days/Minutes
Productivity	3-6% Increase	30-50% Increase
Purchase Cost	5% Reduction	30-50% Reduction

Figure 1--The New Standards

reward for the winners is greenbacks (or yen or marks!). And now the race has a decidedly international flavor, which means that winning means performing to World Class standards.

Remember Roger Bannister?

Remember a few years back when Roger Bannister ran a mile in four minutes? A four-minute mile! A new World Class standard! It seemed incredible--Roger Bannister's story was on television and in the newspapers, and we shook our heads in awe at the achievement.

Suppose you run a four-minute mile today. Will your name be up in lights and whispered by sports commentators? Of course not. Run a four-minute mile today, and you might get a ribbon at a high school track meet. Anything wrong with Roger Bannister? No, of course not. At the time he ran the four-minute mile, that was the standard, the World Class level of excellence. But, since then, the standard for excellence hasn't stood still.

In fact, the high bar has risen. We're able to achieve

more now than we ever would have believed possible just a few short years ago.

The same is true in business.

How do the Customers decide the winner? It's deceptively simple. The newspaper article identified the answer...quality.

Phil Crosby defines quality as conformance to requirements. I'd like to suggest we slightly modify this definition:

"Quality Is Conformance To Expectations."

The winner is the company that meets (or exceeds) the customers' expectations.

The key element in the competitive strategy should be to consistently meet the customers' expectations. But what are they?

The customer expects:
- A product that works
- Value for his dollar
- Products delivered when needed
- To receive what he ordered
- Reliable information
- No hassle!

Of course, these expectations aren't new. What is new is the level of these expectations. Remember when a "high quality" automobile got 20 miles-per-gallon? Today, that's barely a minimum standard. Quality expectations have taken a similar leap. Reaching the new expectations requires an almost defect-free manufacturing process...achieving unprecedented levels of quality often measured in rejects-per-million, as opposed to the old standard of two-to-three percent scrap rates, or 98 percent yield. And the expectations go far beyond flawless product performance.

Customers expect value, paying a fair price and still feeling they are getting a real "deal." However, charging a fair price and still making a reasonable profit means it's cost reduction time! And that cost reduction doesn't mean the usual two-to-three percent annual improvement, either. World Class performance means double-digit improvements, 20-30 percent or better.

Delivery when needed means just that. Customers expect the product on the dock on the day or hour they need it, not within a week or month! Customers are now expecting reliable delivery, helping them avoid excess inventories to cushion unreliable supplier deliveries. At the same time, these customers typically don't know what they'll need weeks or months in advance. This all means that winning the Competitive Race requires quick response to satisfy changing needs of customers. This translates into short manufacturing and purchasing lead times. We're talking lead times of days and minutes, not weeks and months.

All this adds up to a need to focus on a very specific Mission to win the Competitive Race:

The Mission is a nice goal, almost like a policy statement. But a policy statement without an action plan is meaningless. How do we accomplish this Mission?

There have been a number of solutions proposed. We could:

--Out-source. Have our manufacturing done in Third World countries where labor is cheaper.

--Go for wage concessions. If we could negotiate "give-back" programs in our new labor contracts, maybe we wouldn't have to out-source.

--Seek government intervention. When in doubt, ask Uncle Sam to bail us out.

--Blindly invest in robots and automation. After all, haven't we all read that the heart of our problem is our rusting, out-of-date factories?

While attractive on the surface, each one of those proposed solutions is really a trap in disguise. Sure, we can out-source, but what we're really doing is exporting jobs and dollars to another country. What if everybody out-sourced? Those wages and that spending power is lost forever.

Wage concessions certainly sound good. Everyone who wants his salary cut, step to the front. Wage concessions always sound good as long as it's not your wages on the chopping block. But, realistically, wage concessions ultimately face the same drawbacks as out-sourcing--lost purchasing power. In the early days of the automobile industry, Henry Ford walked into his plant one day and gave all his workers a $1-an-hour raise. Did he do it because he was in a good humor that particular day, or because he had money burning a hole in his pocket? No, he did it because the workers, with that extra money, would buy automobiles--Ford automobiles. Our standard of living is dependent on our jobs and our factories.

Government intervention is always popular. It's a little harder to find a case where government intervention has worked as promised. In fact, it's a lot easier to find cases where intervention has done more harm than good. Is that a risk we want to take?

Robots and automation, of course, are the trendy solutions these days. "Automate or evaporate" is a slogan we hear more and more. Tear down the rusty factories, spend a few million in cute robots and computerized assembly lines and get rid of all those pesky employees. For some industries, automation makes a lot of sense; for many others, it makes no sense at all. Can we really afford to scrap our existing factories and make those kinds of capital investments? Do we really have to? Some think not.

While reporting record profits for 1986, a Ford spokesman noted, "Our approach has been that there are times when technology isn't the best answer. Maybe just reorganizing the way you do things can work just as well." David Cole, director of the Office for the Study of Automotive Transportation, concurs. "General Motors was stunned when they achieved Japanese-like efficiency at their NUMMI plant (a Toyota joint-venture) with careful management rather than exotic automation," he says.

To one degree or the other, the above solutions will

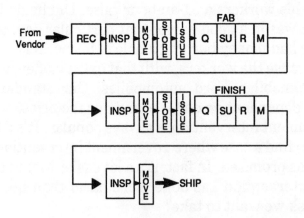

Figure 2--The Typical Manufacturing Process

work. But what these four solutions have in common is they cater to a quick-fix mentality. Not only can we overcome years of neglect or complacency, but we can do it this afternoon! It's easy to be tempted by quick fixes. How many quick fixes, though, have you run across that worked as advertised? Already, major American companies are re-evaluating the quick fix. Do these approaches even address the real problems? In fact, they don't.

Our quest for achieving the Mission begins with an assessment...looking at our current practices and seeking out obstacles in the path to achieving the Mission.

Business As Usual

Let's look at a typical manufacturing process (Figure 2, previous page) and see if we can find some of these obstacles.

Material arrives from the vendor. We receive it, inspect it, store it, eventually issue it to Fabrication (hopefully before it's obsolete or lost!). Once issued to Fabrication, it waits in queue (Q). Eventually, the equipment is set up (SU), the item is run (R) and moved (M) to the next operation. The fabrication step may be called mixing, intermediate production, or various other names in different companies. Several of these Fabrication steps may be working in parallel or series. After leaving Fabrication, the material is inspected, moved to another storage area and eventually moved into a Finishing (or assembly, packaging, or whatever your company calls it) process. Some processing type operations may have even combined Fabrication and Finishing into one continuous step. Once finished, the product is shipped to the customer, warehouses or a sister plant.

Adding Cost, Not Value

Most of the boxes represent steps that add cost, not value, detract from defect-free production and slow down reaction time. It takes a long time to get through the process. For example, if we discover quality problems in final inspection, by the time we communicate those problems back up through the chain, the people who did the original work may not even work there any more!

Because it takes so long to get material through manufacturing and even longer to get material from the suppliers, we're too slow in responding to customer needs. Each inspection, storage and movement means more cost with no value added to the product.

Each of the boxes represent specific obstacles in the path of accomplishing the Mission. The direction to aim our efforts is clear--remove or minimize unwanted steps.

Bill Boyst, from Northern Telecom, came up with a succinct objective. "Do as little as possible," Bill said. "But what you must do, do 100 percent right, 100 percent of the time." Fewer things to do means fewer chances for mistakes.

What we'd like to achieve is the Ideal Manufacturing Process--receive raw material in the morning and ship finished product in the afternoon.

No wasted motion!

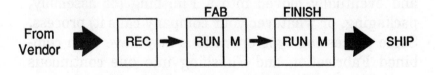

Figure 3--The Ideal Manufacturing Process

What's one of the first things we can eliminate to bring us closer to the Ideal Process? How about the receiving inspection operation? But wait a minute--before we eliminate the receiving inspection, let's consider why we have it in the first place.

Well, it's because the world is full of crooks, people making shoddy products and trying to palm the stuff off on us. They're called suppliers! But who are the suppliers? We are suppliers, and we're really nice folks. Actually, the truth is, all these years our suppliers have been giving us exactly what they thought we ordered. The only person who really understood the specifications we gave the supplier was the person who wrote the specs...and he never talked to the vendor.

Before we can eliminate receiving inspections, we need open lines of communication with our vendors. We must clearly communicate our requirements.

Let's look at another obstacle to moving toward the Ideal Process--storage. Why do we have the storage in the first place?

As it turns out, there are lots of reasons for storage. It compensates for uncertainties in:

- Vendor delivery
- Vendor quality
- Product requirements
- Inventory record accuracy
- Bill of material accuracy
- Minimum quantity purchases
- Material shortages
- Maximize fabrication output
- Costing system
- Performance measurement systems
- EOQs in fabrication

Obviously, we can't just bring in the bulldozers and knock down a couple of warehouses. The first thing we have to do is address all those uncertainties that led to the storage. And you'll notice those uncertainties aren't just confined to Manufacturing.

The Typical process evolved not because of the way we chose to manufacture the product, but as a result of the way we chose to run our businesses. Therefore, moving from Typical to Ideal means more than rearranging the shop floor. It means changing the way we run the business.

A Question For The Future

The question for the 1980s, as we've moved into a world market, is how can we become more competitive and simultaneously see better bottom-line results?

But what happens when we make even small changes in the way we run our businesses? What happens if we're able to do away with inspection on 40 percent of the incoming materials or cut the storage of the raw materials and purchased materials by 40 percent? What happens is we have made a major positive step toward meeting the new competitive standards. It's easy to fall victim to the "all or nothing" syndrome. Slip off your diet for a quick candy bar, and, what the heck, might as well scrap the whole thing. Bring on the ice cream and cookies! The all or nothing syndrome doesn't take into account that each small improvement in the manufacturing process translates into dollars, sometimes big dollars, or other critical resources saved. We might, for instance, never be able to eliminate all inspections or do away with all storage, but each incremental change brings us closer to our goal. To borrow a phrase from Just-In-Time, we want continuous improvement.

Now, is this MRP II, JIT, TQC or what? Is some other acronym the key to eliminating the obstacles and approaching the Ideal Process?

The Right Question

We're asking the wrong question. The question is not which acronym we should use or which gets the credit. The question is, "Are we applying the right--or best--approaches to overcome the major hurdles on the way to the Ideal?" Let's examine some of those approaches more closely.

MRP II is a proven approach for managing resources to run a manufacturing business. It focuses on such items as:
- Accurate records
- Long-range visibility
- Valid and integrated plans
- Stable master schedule
- Valid schedules
- On-time deliveries

Without valid and integrated plans, without accuracy in inventory, the bills of material and routings, without a valid master schedule, we're going to be left at the starting gate. But do you have to accomplish every item on the MRP II list to get better? Of course not. If you can only achieve 95 percent inventory record accuracy, 98 percent bill of material accuracy and unload an overloaded master schedule, you will be better off than before. Much better off, in fact. When we do all of the MRP II items well, it's called "Class A."

JIT is one of the hottest imports from Japan. In many areas it challenges the way we've always done business. JIT focuses in on such areas as:
- Product and component quality

- Lot size reduction
- Set-up reduction
- Lead time reduction
- WIP reduction
- Vendor reliability
- People involvement
- Paperwork/transaction reduction

JIT looks toward simplifying the manufacturing process to gain faster response times and higher quality. Do we need to do everything on this list to get better? No. We can reduce set-up times and shorten manufacturing lead times without ever tackling the question of vendor reliability.

If we are going to be excellent, if we are going to be World Class, we are going to have to accomplish everything on these two lists and several other lists as well. We are going to have to become "Class A" MRP II users and the equivalent of "Class A" JIT users. We are going to have to tackle the question of quality and of the "thinking worker." These are not optional activities--these are necessities.

It's easy to see how the MRP II activities and the JIT activities items are locked together. With MRP II, we know that inventory and bill of material accuracy are necessary for valid schedules in the factory. In JIT, a reliable, defect-free manufacturing process is a prerequisite to minimizing work-in-process (WIP), thus minimizing manufacturing lead times.

What we need to recognize is the interdependence of the groups themselves. Imagine MRP II as a circle, JIT as a circle, TQC as a circle. In the past, we have seen those circles as separate islands of activities to focus on independently. There's the MRP II solution, the JIT solution, the TQC solution--lots of separate solutions, separate is-

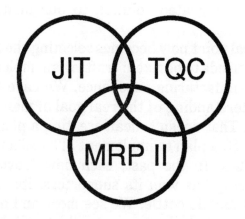

Figure 4--The Overlapping Circles Of World Class

lands. It has become increasingly obvious, though, that those circles are overlapping. In fact, the circles approach being concentric, all parts of a single overall solution.

For example, one of the goals of JIT is a reduction of WIP. Yet the way to achieve reduced WIP requires the visibility of valid capacity plans, a goal of MRP II. It's hard to imagine how we can expect vendors to reliably deliver with short lead times without giving them visibility of future requirements. MRP II provides long-range visibility, so suppliers and the shop floor know what to expect. Since they know what's coming, vendors are able to supply smaller lots, a goal of JIT. Because smaller lots are being run, there's a faster feedback loop, which helps improve quality--a goal of TQC.

Integrated Manufacturing

We need to go beyond the acronyms and see the "common parts" in MRP II, JIT and TQC. We then need to provide an integrated solution to our manufacturing problems.

The critical point now becomes selecting the right tools to fix what needs to be fixed: crafting an implementation plan for manufacturing excellence. We have to develop a basic understanding of the real goal of manufacturing excellence. That doesn't mean creating a plan to implement MRP II, a plan to implement JIT and a plan to implement TQC. In the past, each new "revolution" in manufacturing has won its supporters, its champions, who go out and do battle. We see more and more internal "wars" over which acronym will prevail. We recently visited a company where the Quality team and the MRP II team were fighting over who got to conduct a vendor education program! After all, people involvement at every level is the major common part!

Executive management is often confused about which acronym they should rally around. Unfortunately, too often they just let the different factions slug it out, hoping the strongest and best will rise to the top. It's survival of the fittest! And who suffers in a situation like this? Of course, it's the workers, struggling to keep the ship afloat while the guys in ties duke it out. While we argue over acronyms, we overlook our most valuable resource--our people. Instead of bringing them in on the quest for excellence, we leave them confused and frustrated. It appears that three or four different programs have been thrust on them, all requiring their valuable time. There aren't enough hours in the day to do justice to the avalanche of acronyms. Instead of becoming our partners in meeting the World Class standards, our people adopt a wait-and-see attitude.

Where To Next?

The first stage is assessing where your company is-- focusing on the problems outstanding.

Much in the same way a financial audit gauges your company's financial health, you need a manufacturing audit to gauge both your company's current status and the areas where work is needed. That's important, because you need to know which approaches to look to first. Next, you need a viable action plan to make the necessary changes a reality. Education is an important part of that plan.

World competition is getting tougher every day. Our challenge as educators is to not stop searching for the best solution, the best road to excellence.

Look beyond the acronyms! *Absorb what is useful, and excellence will follow.*

Linking People To Progress

By Dave Garwood

Grinding away and getting nowhere."

That's how one key executive in a manufacturing business recently described the results of the past year's efforts as his company tried to implement new systems to help run their business better.

The efforts weren't totally in vain, but the results fell far short of their expectations. Disappointment and frustration showed on everyone's face. The fruits of their efforts weren't showing up on the bottom line.

What causes the problem? Lack of education and training? No company, in my experience, has ever tried to implement new programs without education and training.

The real issue is whether the education program focused on the critical issues and achieved the desired results.

Right Road, Wrong Path

When introducing change into any organization, there's a normal distribution, a bell curve, of attitudes about the change. Five percent of the people are super-enthused and confident. They're the "Rambos" of the organization. Another five percent are also confident, but in the opposite direction..."It'll never work here, and we'll see to it" is their assessment.

Between the two extremes is the Silent Majority...the 90 percent of the company who have both the skills and expertise to make the new ideas work, but have a skeptical "wait and see" outlook. With arms folded, they politely nod their heads "yes" when asked if they will support the new efforts and believe they will be effective. They slowly shake their heads "no" when asked if they have questions or concerns. When the meeting is over, what do they do? Walk away and go back to "business as usual."

Yet the success (or failure) of the new program is in their hands. The Silent Majority is a hardworking, dedicated group. They have a wealth of knowledge about what needs to change and how to do it.

So why is the Silent Majority not enthusiastically embracing the new ideas and charging ahead to implement them?

There are several reasons, some very simple, some equally complex.

For a start, some of the Silent Majority don't understand how the new ideas work. No one ever explained it to them. Others question if these new ideas really apply to their business. Some have seen many new programs come and go, and they've come to believe the new ideas will eventually die on the vine, lacking management support. Others don't see the connection between their problems and frustrations and the new ideas being proposed. They question whether the whole effort is worthwhile.

The solution to the Silent Majority dilemma is more complex than simply teaching a few formulas, new terminology or techniques. Yet that's what we associate with the word "education." We have found programs that focus only on "education" won't solve the Silent Majority's problem.

To implement the changes we must make to become a World Class Competitor, we must change old habits, attitudes and mindsets that are deeply ingrained.

Learning what to do and doing it aren't the same! Everyone knows that seat belts can save lives. So no one ever drives without their seat belt fastened, right? And since we all know that losing weight requires a sensible diet and regular exercise, none of us have the least bit of trouble losing that ten pounds, right?

Wrong. Very wrong. Knowing isn't the same as doing.

Most so-called Education Programs are focused on acquiring knowledge, but are weak on overcoming the reasons for the apathy. A process that goes beyond education is essential to turn the Silent Majority into an enthusiastic, vocal majority that's ready to seize the ownership for implementing change in their company. An effective Education Program to bring about change should include these five basic characteristics:

1) Clearly Identify the Mission

MRP II, JIT and TQC Project Teams can turn into dueling banjos, each snatching the lead from each other until the audience--everyone else in the factory--is exhausted and confused. While the acronyms are playing their own tunes, the majority of employees are trying to figure out what the real point is.

Why are the new programs needed?

The first step is to explain why! Why do we need to run the business differently? What do we expect to accomplish with the new programs? The answer is simple. Keeping the company at the front of the Competitive

Race is getting tougher.

Who decides the winner of the Competitive Race? Customers! Customers award blue ribbons to those companies that meet or exceed their expectations. Customers expect defect-free products delivered on time. They want value, to feel they got a good deal. The expectations aren't new. But the level of those expectations is much higher. It's a global market today, with tougher competition that has raised the high bar. Therefore, the Mission is to focus, a single focus, on meeting World Class Performance Standards in high quality, low cost and quick response. Every obstacle in the path of meeting this Mission is the target. Some of those obstacles are created by old ways of running the business.

2) Visible Management Actions

Doubts about management support is the most frequently voiced reason we hear for hesitancy and lack of enthusiasm to implement new ideas. Is lack of support a fact or a misperception? Doesn't matter. It's the perception that counts! Bringing in outside experts, sending letters claiming to be supportive and spending $25,000 doesn't create the perception of support.

When executives skip education sessions, any doubts about management support are removed. Their absence sends a clear message. They confirm this new effort has low priority. If it was really important, they'd be in the front row.

And who is management? One fellow in class quickly replied, "Everyone above me!" Visible actions must come from every level in the organization. The responsibility isn't reserved only for the top. "Lead by example" should be the motto at all levels.

3) Total Involvement

Including only a select view of what the new program is all about sends a damaging message to the rest of the troops. "We don't need your help."

Concentrating attendees from Manufacturing implies that the problem is a manufacturing department problem. As we move to place responsibility for quality at the source, or create work cells or clean up inventory record accuracy, every department from Accounting to the Shop Floor will be affected.

For the program to succeed, we need to involve everyone right at the beginning. We can't afford to leave anyone out because we need everyone pulling on the rope.

4) Focus on Interactive Discussion

Quite often, programs are structured to discourage, not encourage, discussion. Who is going to raise a question or concern with the outside expert in the room and risk looking stupid? How can we have a meaningful discussion in a room of 50-75 people? The unstated objective during a Saturday or late-evening session is to finish on time and get out of there as soon as possible. If a Training Director serves as the Discussion Leader, he or she lacks the credibility (and possibly the knowledge) necessary to answer vital questions.

Changing the Silent Majority requires creating an atmosphere where people feel comfortable about expressing their fears, concerns and uncertainties. Here are a few key elements we recommend you consider for the interactive discussions:

- Small groups (20 people or less)

- Mix people from various departments
- Limit each discussion session to a maximum of two hours
- Focus each session on a specific topic
- Discussion Leader should be a peer, not an outsider
- Dedicate most of the time to discussion, not technical explanations
- Create examples of how concepts apply to your products

5) Follow a Structured Program

Grabbing the latest brochure from the "In" box and sending people to outside seminars is a classic mistake.

While informative, each seminar usually has a narrow focus...looking only at MRP II or JIT or TQC or CIM or...

The company objective and plans after the seminar must be clear. The problem is compounded when the Rambos try to inject their newfound wealth of wisdom into the veins of a privileged few in the company during a couple of Saturday and late evening sessions.

Thumbing through a catalog of disjointed courses and allowing people to pick courses with little direction other than the length or location of a course can be an expensive proposition. Purchasing video tapes and bringing in outside consultants for training without laying out a structured program can become a sizable investment with little return. An organized program with clear objectives for each step can save time and money.

A Jumpstart

The aftermath of this hit-or-miss hodgepodge approach reminds me of a car battery on a cold morning. It grinds away, but doesn't have enough spark to get the car moving. A jumpstart is the answer, a quick charge to help them pick up the pace and get moving toward World Class Performance. After having been involved with many companies faced with this problem, we have developed a proven program, called **Operation Jumpstart**. The program is organized to ensure the objective is clearly defined and communicated, management actions are visible and all levels and every department in the organization are involved. The program focuses on the application of the new ideas to your products.

The first step is to get an Executive Group and a Core Team away from the company for a comprehensive overview. They learn what World Class Performance means and to integrate MRP II, JIT, TQC, CIM and a potpourri of other acronyms into a program with a single focus. By getting away from the company, they're not distracted. Because they mix and interact with people from other companies, they learn that their problems are very similar (or even the same!). A common understanding, clear direction, confidence and enthusiasm for getting started is the result. The focus shifts from acronyms to business issues. Executives from every major function participate to ensure a total company effort. The Core Team is comprised of key people from all departments.

Life after the seminars is the hard part. A series of meetings is organized to discuss how the ideas apply in their business, the potential benefits and the hurdles they'll have to overcome. Implementation plans begin to evolve. The Executive Group meets once a week for a couple of hours for two months. The Core Team meets three or four times a week for a couple of months. The Executive Group meeting is another visible action, reinforcing their commitment. These meetings are focused on changing the way we run the business, thus the term

"Business Meetings."

Each Business Meeting is 20 percent understanding concepts and techniques and 80 percent applying the ideas and measuring results.

Each meeting focuses on a specific topic. For example, one session might be on reducing lead times. Learning why shorter lead times are better may take 20 minutes. The next hour is centered around how to overcome the obstacles to smaller lot sizes and recognize the potential benefits. Plans to attack the problem begin to take shape. As individuals from various departments see that other people are making changes and cooperating to help them out, teamwork becomes a reality, not a slogan. Interdepartmental barriers come down. Communication opens up. Confidence increases. Enthusiasm builds up.

Other meetings may focus on master scheduling, Kanban, eliminating inspection operations, vendor partnerships, lot size reductions, bill of material structuring, capacity planning, and so forth. The number of meetings required is a function of the number of topics that need to be discussed.

Next, the Core Team spreads their newfound confidence and enthusiasm to a Critical Mass...a group of informal leaders and opinionmakers in the organization. The Critical Mass goes through the same Business Meeting format, again, in small groups. One size program doesn't fit all. The makeup of the Executive Group, Core Teams and Critical Mass and the topics required all need to be tailored to fit each company.

Eventually, the discussions expand to the balance of the Silent Majority. The result of Operation Jumpstart is total involvement at all levels in all departments in the company. Understanding where the company is headed and why is clear.

Not A Pep Rally

Pep rallies, quick fixes and shortcuts won't do it. Bringing in a cheerleader, holding a couple of big meetings and expecting people to change how they do their jobs overnight is unrealistic. If your implementation efforts are frustrating and disappointing, a jumpstart (to restart!) may be just what you need.

Change takes time and involvement. Delegating responsibility for that change to outsiders is doomed for failure. It's an inside job. It takes leadership. And that leadership starts at the top and moves down through every level in the organization. No one is immune.

We have learned that poor quality, not high quality, is expensive. Taking the time to make sure everyone is in tune with the changes we need to make is not expensive. *Not taking the time is expensive!*

To order more copies of A Jumpstart To World Class Performance, or to request back issues of Hot List II, please contact:

R.D. Garwood, Inc.
P.O. Box 28755
Atlanta, GA 30358-0755
(404) 952-2976

Please call for prices, as discounts are available for bulk purchasers. To be placed on the **Hot List II** mailing list, please send your business card to the above address.